The Little Big Book for
Grandfathers

Edited by ALICE WONG and HIRO CLARK WAKABAYASHI
Designed by TIMOTHY SHANER and CHRISTOPHER MEASOM

welcome
BOOKS
NEW YORK · SAN FRANCISCO

Published in 2005 by Welcome Books®
An imprint of Welcome Enterprises, Inc.
6 West 18th Street, New York, NY 10011
(212) 989-3200; Fax (212) 989-3205
www.welcomebooks.com

Publisher: Lena Tabori
Project Director: Alice Wong
Designers: Timothy Shaner and Christopher Measom
Project Assistant: Deidra Garcia
Tales and Legends retold by Deidra Garcia and Alice Wong
Recipes and Activities Text by Monique Peterson
Line Illustrations for Activities by Sarah Kaplan

Front jacket illustration by Jessie Willcox Smith

Distributed to the trade in the U.S. and Canada by Andrews McMeel Distribution Services
U.S. Order Department and Customer Service Toll-free: (800) 943-9839
U.S. Orders-only Fax: (800) 943-9831; PUBNET S&S San Number: 200-2442
Canada Orders Toll-free: (800) 268-3216; Canada Order-only Fax: (888) 849-8151

Library of Congress Cataloging-in-Publication Data on file.

ISBN 1-932183-71-X

Printed in China

FIRST EDITION

1 3 5 7 9 10 8 6 4 2

Contents

Contents

Contents

Foreword

When Welcome published *The Little Big Book for Moms* in May 2000, we received calls and letters from many fans asking for more. We followed with editions for dads, grandmothers, girls, and boys in the Little Big Book series. The e-mails and notes kept coming, now asking specifically: "What about grandfathers?" One fan in particular argued that there are countless books for grandmothers but few for grandfathers, and that *really*, it is grandfathers who spend the most time with the children while grandmothers cook.

I know this to be true. In fact, I just spent a weekend with my in-laws during which Granddad was wiggling his ears, flipping his eyelids (yuck!), and flaring his nostrils for the amusement of the children while Grandma was busy with dinner. That is our weekend routine at my in-laws' house in Bucks County, Pennsylvania. My children and nephew are always off with Granddad looking for bugs and bird nests, hammering and building, digging for potatoes or roasting nuts for dinner and snacks, reading a book, or listening and dancing to old favorite songs—while Grandma is shopping for and preparing meals.

We knew that grandfathers rightly deserved a Little Big Book to share with their grandchildren. The problem was that we packed so much in the other books of the series, we were fearful of not coming up with enough good, fresh material. But we decided to try and, well ... just look at the list

Foreword

of contents on pages 4 through 7! The "Legendary Tall Tales" are a brilliant addition to this series. Grandfathers will enjoy reading the fantastic tales of the mighty Paul Bunyan, Wild Bill Hickock, and other great legends from America's past. We selected the "Literary Excerpts" passages, about life, wisdom, and time, from favorite classics. For example, Oz shares his thoughts on brains, heart, and courage in *The Wonderful Wizard of Oz*; and the fox teaches about friendship in *The Little Prince*. We also found much wisdom in our favorite Aesop's fables, as well as some wonderful poetry included here.

Other titles in The Little Big Book series contain a wealth of fairy tales and nursery rhymes. This book presents favorites with a bit of a twist. There are fun accounts of how the nursery rhymes "The Cat and the Fiddle" and "Four and Twenty Blackbirds" came to be, as well as the retelling of well-loved fairy tales in short verse. And after all that reading, Granddad can sing an old-time song or tell a funny joke, roll up his sleeves, and dig in to an activity or recipe. Try some of my family's favorites: Capture a Spider Web and Tiny Boats, or Kitchen-Sink Pizzas and Taco Temptations.

Thank you all for your support. We happily envision your families enjoying the wonderful years of childhood with well-used and well-loved copies of our books for moms, dads, grandmothers—and now, grandfathers. Please don't stop sending us your thoughts and suggestions.

—*Alice Wong, Editor*

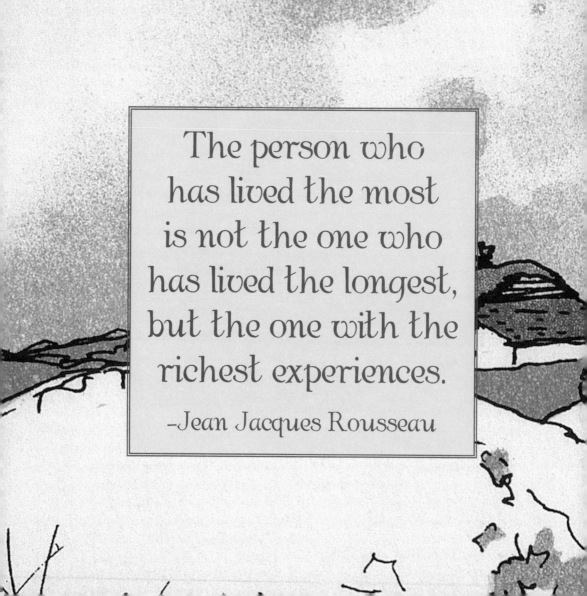

The person who
has lived the most
is not the one who
has lived the longest,
but the one with the
richest experiences.

-Jean Jacques Rousseau

The Cat and the Fiddle

by L. Frank Baum

Perhaps you think this verse is all nonsense, and that the things it mentions could never have happened; but they did happen, as you will understand when I have explained them all to you clearly.

Little Bobby was the only son of a small farmer who lived out of town upon a country road. Bobby's mother looked after the house and Bobby's father took care of the farm, and Bobby himself, who was not very big, helped them both as much as he was able.

It was lonely upon the farm, especially when his father and mother were both busy at work, but the boy had one way to amuse himself that served to pass many an hour when he would not otherwise have known what to do. He was very fond of music, and his father one day brought him from the town a small fiddle, or violin,

Hey, diddle, diddle,
The cat and the fiddle,
The cow jumped
over the moon!
The little dog laughed
To see such sport,
And the dish ran off
with the spoon!

which he soon learned to play upon. I don't suppose he was a very fine musician, but the tunes he played pleased himself, as well as his father and mother, and Bobby's fiddle soon became his constant companion.

One day in the warm summer the farmer and his wife determined to drive to the town to sell their butter and eggs and bring back some groceries in exchange for them, and while they were

14

gone Bobby was to be left alone.

"We shall not be back till late in the evening," said his mother, "for the weather is too warm to drive very fast. But I have left you a dish of bread and milk for your supper, and you must be a good boy and amuse yourself with your fiddle until we return."

Bobby promised to be good and look after the house, and then his father and mother climbed into the wagon and drove away to the town.

The boy was not entirely alone, for there was the big black tabby-cat lying upon the floor in the kitchen, and the little yellow dog barking at the wagon as it drove away, and the big moolie-cow lowing in the pasture down by the brook. Animals are often very good company, and Bobby did not feel nearly as lonely as he would had there been no living thing about the house.

Besides he had some work to do in the garden, pulling up the weeds that grew thick in the car-rotbed, and when the last faint sounds of the wheels had died away he went into the garden and began his task.

The little dog went too, for dogs love to be with people and to watch what is going on; and he sat down near Bobby and cocked up his ears and wagged his tail and seemed to take a great interest in the weeding. Once in a while he would rush away to chase a butterfly or bark at a beetle that crawled through the garden, but he always came back to the boy and kept near his side.

By and by the cat, which found it lonely in the big, empty kitchen, now that Bobby's mother was gone, came walking into the garden also, and lay down upon a path in the sunshine and lazily watched the boy at his work. The dog and the cat were good friends, having lived together so long that they did not care to fight each other. To be sure Towser, as the little dog was called, sometimes tried to tease pussy, being himself very mischievous; but when the cat put out her sharp claws and showed her teeth, Towser, like a wise little dog, quickly ran away, and so they managed to get along in a friendly manner.

By the time the carrot-bed was all weeded, the sun was sinking behind the edge of the forest and the new moon rising in the east, and now Bobby began to feel hungry and went into the house for his dish of bread and milk.

"I think I'll take my supper down to the brook," he said to himself, "and sit upon the grassy bank while I eat it. And I'll take my fiddle, too, and play upon it to pass the time until father and mother come home."

It was a good idea, for down by the brook it was cool and pleasant; so Bobby took his fiddle under his arm and carried his dish of bread and milk down to the bank that sloped to the edge of the brook. It was rather a steep

bank, but Bobby sat upon the edge, and placing his fiddle beside him, leaned against a tree and began to eat his supper.

The little dog had followed at his heels, and the cat also came slowly walking after him, and as Bobby ate, they sat one on either side of him and looked earnestly into his face as if they too were hungry. So he threw some of the bread to Towser, who grabbed it eagerly and swallowed it in the twinkling of an eye. And Bobby left some of the milk in the dish for the cat, also, and she came lazily up and drank it in a dainty, sober fashion, and licked both the dish and spoon until no drop of the milk was left.

Then Bobby picked up his fiddle and tuned it and began to play some of the pretty tunes he knew. And while he played he watched the moon rise higher and higher until it was reflected in the smooth, still water of the brook. Indeed, Bobby could not tell which was

17

the plainest to see, the moon in the sky or the moon in the water. The little dog lay quietly on one side of him, and the cat softly purred upon the other, and even the moolie-cow was attracted by the music and wandered near until she was browsing the grass at the edge of the brook.

After a time, when Bobby had played all the tunes he knew, he laid the fiddle down beside him, near to where the cat slept, and then he lay down upon the bank and began to think.

It is very hard to think long upon a dreamy summer night without falling asleep, and very soon Bobby's eyes closed and he forgot all about the dog and the cat and the cow and the fiddle, and dreamed he was Jack the Giant Killer and was just about to slay the biggest giant I the world.

And while he dreamed, the cat sat up and yawned and stretched herself, and then began wagging her long tail from side to side and watching the moon that was reflected in the water.

But the fiddle lay just behind her, and as she moved her tail, she drew it between the strings of the fiddle, where it caught fast. Then she gave her tail a jerk and pulled the fiddle against the tree, which made a loud noise. This frightened the cat greatly, and not knowing what was the matter with her tail, she started to run as fast as she could. But still the fiddle clung to her tail, and at every step it bounded along and made such a noise that she screamed with terror. And in her fright she ran straight towards the cow, which, seeing a black streak coming at her, and hearing the racket made by the fiddle, became also frightened and made such a jump to get out of the way that she jumped right across the brook, leaping over the very spot where the moon shone in the water!

Bobby had been awakened by the noise, and opened his eyes in

The Cat and the Fiddle

time to see the cow jump; and at first it seemed to him that she had actually jumped over the moon in the sky, instead of the one in the brook.

The dog was delighted at the sudden excitement caused by the cat, and ran barking and dancing along the bank, so that he presently knocked against the dish, and behold! it slid down the bank, carrying the spoon with it, and fell with a splash into the water of the brook.

As soon as Bobby recovered from his surprise he ran after the cat, which had raced to the house, and soon came to where the fiddle lay upon the ground, it having at last dropped from the cat's tail. He examined it carefully, and was glad to find it was not hurt, in spite of its rough usage. And then he had to go across the brook and drive the cow back over the little bridge, and also to roll up his sleeve and reach into the water to recover the dish and the spoon.

Then he went back to the house and lighted a lamp, and sat down to compose a new tune before his father and mother returned.

The cat had recovered from her fright and lay quietly under the stove, and Towser sat upon the floor panting, with his mouth wide open, and looking so comical that Bobby thought he was actually laughing at the whole occurrence.

And these were the words to the tune that Bobby composed that night:

Hey, diddle, diddle,
The cat and the fiddle,
The cow jumped
over the moon!
The little dog laughed
To see such sport,
And the dish ran away
with the spoon!

ACTIVITIES

Noisemakers

"*Children should be seen and not heard*" *is a time-honored saying. But sometimes it's fun to cut loose and make as much noise as possible along with your grandkids! You can make simple whistles and kazoos from perfectly ordinary items like paper, grass, combs, and toilet-paper rolls. Create a homemade orchestra and organize a whirlwind musical tour all around the house.*

WHISTLING GRASS

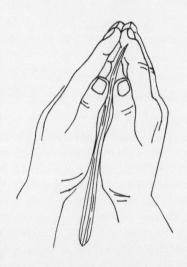

Find a wide, unbroken blade of grass about as long as your finger. Hold the blade of grass between your thumbs by pressing the flat sides of the grass with the sides of your thumbs. Your other fingers should be held in loose fists, and your thumbnails should be facing you. There should be a small gap, between the first and second joints on your thumbs, where you can see the blade of grass. Make sure the grass is stretched tightly across this gap. Put your lips to the hole and blow. You should make a high piercing whistle. If you're not getting a sound, try stretching the grass tighter or finding a broader blade.

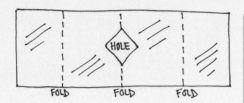

COMB WARBLER

Fold a piece of tissue paper over a medium-size hair comb. Place your lips against the comb and sing or hum to create a truly weird sound and tickling sensation.

KAZOO

Take a square of waxed paper and cover one end of an empty toilet paper roll. Secure the waxed paper with tape or a rubber band and make two slits in it. Hum through the open end of the tube to create a kazoo-like sound.

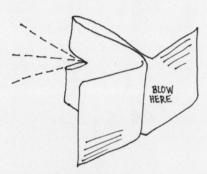

PAPER WHISTLE

Fold a piece of paper in half and cut a hole at the middle of the fold. Now, fold each side back so there is a crease facing you (*see above*). Hold your lips against the front crease and blow to produce an ear-splitting whistle!

I come from Alabama with my banjo on my knee,
I'm goin' to Lou'siana, my true love for to see.

Oh! Susanna, Oh, don't you cry for me,
I've come from Alabama with my banjo on my knee.

It rained all night the day I left, the weather it was dry,
The sun so hot I froze to death! Susanna don't you cry.

Oh! Susanna, Oh, don't you cry for me,
I've come from Alabama with my banjo on my knee.

Oh! Susanna

LEGENDARY TALL TALES: PECOS BILL RIDES AGAIN

Pecos Bill was the greatest cowboy who ever lived. His adventures started way back when he was just a little critter. When Pecos was a baby, his family decided to pack up their wagon and head out West. Pecos had many brothers and sisters, so his mom and dad knew they'd have to find a place that was big enough to handle their family. Traveling on the wagon trail was rough, but Pecos didn't mind. At one stop they made, Pecos's mother put him down for a nap in the shade of a tree. Just then, a huge bear came stomping out of the woods. Pecos's family took one look, jumped back in their wagon, and high-tailed it out of there as fast as they could! Unfortunately, with all the kids around, they forgot about little Pecos, still asleep under that tree.

Pecos could have been in a lot of trouble, but luckily for him, a passing wolf noticed the little tyke and decided to adopt him. Pecos took to the wolf life immediately and grew up learning how to survive and have a wild time in the wilderness.

Pecos loved his wolf family, and probably would've stayed with them forever if a passing cowboy hadn't one day noticed him wrestling with his wolf brother.

"Howdy," said the cowboy.

"Howdy," answered Pecos.

"What's a young fella like yourself doing this far out in the wilderness all by his lonesome?"

"'Fella?'" said Pecos. "I'm not a fella. I'm a wolf."

"If you're a wolf, then where's your tail?" asked the cowboy.

Pecos looked down at his rear, but he

couldn't see a tail of any kind. He tried to catch sight of it and spun around and around faster and faster until he was dizzy.

The cowboy laughed. "Now, cut that out before you raise up a sandstorm. You are not a wolf—you're a boy. And if you are a boy, you might as well be a cowboy."

Pecos liked the sound of that. "But what kind of people are cowboys?" he asked.

"Well, we spend our days herding cattle across the open range. Most of us are reasonable folk, but there is one gang of cowboys that are as wild as a bunch of bucking broncos and as crazy as a pack of buzzards!"

This was the Fire Gulch Gang, and the more Pecos Bill heard about them, the more he knew he had to meet them.

After the cowboy had taught him all he knew about being a cowboy, Pecos said good-bye and set off to find the Fire Gulch Gang. It wasn't easy, since they always camped in the wildest, most dangerous parts of the land. Along the way he

fought a giant rattlesnake and a fearsome mountain lion, who after that followed Pecos around like a couple of meek puppy dogs.

Finally, Pecos Bill came upon the Fire Gulch Gang. He marched into their camp and asked, "Who's the leader here?" The leader took one look at the snake around his neck and the ferocious mountain lion by his side and gulped. "I was, but you are now!" And that's how Pecos Bill became leader to the wildest, fiercest gang of cowpunchers the West had ever seen.

Pecos Bill and his gang had many amazing adventures together, and legends grew up around their exploits. A particular feat proved that no one and no *thing* on the planet could escape his lasso. One summer it was so hot that all the rivers and lakes on the prairie dried up. Everyone thought they'd have to move, because there wasn't enough water for the crops and the cattle. But, one day, the gang saw a dark thunder cloud on the horizon. They all cheered since this meant a nice, long thunderstorm would be coming and all the rivers and lakes would fill up again. But then everyone groaned when they saw that the storm was actually turning away from their camp.

"I guess we'll have to move after all," said one cowboy.

"Not if I can help it," Pecos Bill declared. He grabbed a lasso, jumped on his horse, and set off like lightning for the thunderstorm. Now, this wasn't any ordinary thunderstorm, but the biggest, wildest, wettest storm the West had ever seen. Pecos Bill rode up next to it, and then whirled his lasso over his head and hooked it onto the black cloud. Quick as a wink, Pecos was whisked up into the storm, and before he knew it, he was actually riding the wild cloud itself!

That storm almost threw Pecos Bill several times, but Pecos held on with all of his might, and eventually the storm stopped trying to fight so hard. Then, just like a man leading a horse, Pecos directed the storm over all the crops and cattle. The cowboys shouted with joy as the big, fat raindrops started pouring down on them, replenishing all the lakes and rivers. They could just make out Pecos, sitting on top of the black thundercloud, waving his hat and yelling for all he was worth!

Pecos loved his wild trip across the prairie. From then on, whenever life at the camp got a little too slow for him, he'd keep his eye out for a thunderstorm or two. As soon as he spotted one, he'd sneak off with his trusty lasso for another whirlwind ride! 🏃

I've often thought

I've often thought
how nice 'twould be
To gallop through
the sky,

To glide o'er towns
and churches,
And pass the steam
cars by.

But when my horse
begins to "break",
And go to pieces
too,

I've often thought
it would be hard
To see just what
to do.

Reading the Clouds

*C*louds are more than streaks of puffy whiteness that decorate the sky. These massive formations of water vapor bring rain and snow as well as protection from the sun's hot rays. By learning how to recognize different clouds and their formations, you and your grandchildren can practice age-old ways of predicting the weather and staying in touch with nature.

CUMULUS

These puffy cotton-candy clouds are commonly seen against a clear blue summer backdrop of sky. They're a sign of fair weather and are perfect for viewing while lying on your back on a grassy knoll. As they drift lazily across the sky, see what shapes and characters they conjure up for you and your grandchild.

CIRRUS

You'll see thin, wispy, curly cirrus clouds higher in the sky than other clouds, anywhere from three to ten miles overhead. These clouds are made up almost entirely of ice crystals and often signal that a storm is on its way within 18 to 36 hours.

CIRROSTRATUS

High-altitude cirrostratus clouds form large, wispy sheets across the sky. They often look like large zebra stripes, which is a sure indication of bad weather to come. These clouds often loom above thunderheads, so be sure to seek cover if you see them.

STRATUS

The word stratus comes from the word "stratum," which means "layer." This is the name for the flat, thick clouds that hover near the ground. These clouds are mostly made of water droplets but they don't produce rain. If you're stuck in the middle of a stratus cloud, expect to be misted by drizzle.

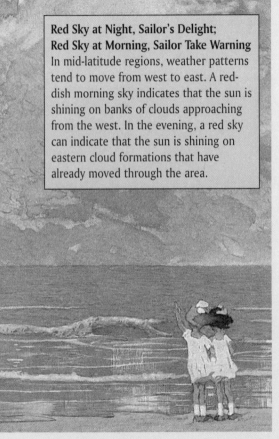

Red Sky at Night, Sailor's Delight;
Red Sky at Morning, Sailor Take Warning
In mid-latitude regions, weather patterns tend to move from west to east. A reddish morning sky indicates that the sun is shining on banks of clouds approaching from the west. In the evening, a red sky can indicate that the sun is shining on eastern cloud formations that have already moved through the area.

NIMBOSTRATUS

These low-hanging, flat clouds are often shapeless but easy to identify because they are darker in color than other clouds. *Nimbus* is the Roman word for rain cloud—so named because the bottoms of these clouds are heavy with falling raindrops or snow.

FOG

The difference between fog and low-lying stratus clouds is that fog touches the surface of the earth. Fog appears when a cold front has moved into an area with warmer air. When the cold and warm air meet, the naturally occurring water vapor in the air condenses into a thick mist. Although fog isn't necessarily an indicator of bad weather, its blinding whiteness can pose a hazard.

A Ring around the Moon
Means a Storm Is Coming Soon
Moon rings are caused by light refracting off the ice crystals in cirrus and cirrostratus clouds. This bright halo around the moon is usually an indicator of an approaching cold front. The brighter the ring, the nearer the storm.

Twenty Little Raindrops

BY MILDRED PLEW MERRYMAN

Twenty little raindrops, laughing out aloud,
Tightly tied their bonnets on and tumbled from a cloud.
Two darted downward to dance from place to place,
Two bounced upon a roof, two ran a race;
But one was very dizzy
From his recent trip so whizzy,
So he met a little bird and washed its face.

Two little raindrops trickled through the trees,
Two preferred excitement so they coasted on the breeze,
Two little raindrops softly sat them down
Plump on the point of a steeple in the town;
But one was very merry
So he lighted on a fairy
And there he sat, a twinkle in her crown.

Twenty little raindrops, laughing out aloud,
Tightly tied their bonnets on and tumbled from a cloud.
Two made a rainbow with a sunset beam,
Three that were daring dove into a running stream,
But one was very lazy
So he crawled into a daisy
And dreamed a little raindrop dream.

THE JUNGLE BOOK
by Rudyard Kipling

It was in the days when Baloo was teaching him the Law of the Jungle. The big, serious, old brown bear was delighted to have so quick a pupil, for the young wolves will only learn as much of the Law of the Jungle as applies to their own pack and tribe, and run away as soon as they can repeat the Hunting-Verse: "Feet that make no noise; eyes that can see in the dark; ears that can hear the winds in their lairs, and sharp white teeth, all these things are the marks of our brothers except Tabaqui the Jackal and the hyena whom we hate." But Mowgli, as man-cub, had to learn a great deal more than this. Sometimes Bagheera the Black Panther would come lounging through the jungle to see how his pet was getting on, and would purr with his head against a tree while Mowgli recited the day's lesson to Baloo. The boy could climb almost as well as he could swim, and swim almost as well as he could run. So Baloo, the Teacher of the Law, taught him the Wood and Water Laws: how to tell a rotten branch from a sound one; how to speak politely to the wild bees when he came upon a hive of them fifty feet above ground; what to say to Mang the Bat when he disturbed him in the branches at mid-day; and how to warn the watersnakes in the pools before he splashed down among them. None of the Jungle-People like being disturbed, and all are very ready to fly at an intruder.

Then, too, Mowgli was taught the Strangers' Hunting-Call, which must be repeated aloud till it is answered, whenever one of the Jungle-People hunts outside his own grounds. It means, translated: "Give me leave to hunt here because I am hungry"; and the answer is: "Hunt then for food, but not for pleasure."

All this will show you how much Mowgli had to learn by heart, and he grew very tired of saying the same thing over a hundred times. But, as Baloo said to Bagheera, one day when Mowgli had been cuffed and run off in a temper. "A man's cub is a man's cub, and he must learn *all* the Law of the Jungle."

"But think how small he is," said the black panther, who would have spoiled Mowgli if he had had his own way. "How can his little head carry all thy long talk?"

"Is there anything in the jungle too little to be killed? No. That is why I teach him these things, and that is why I hit him, very softly, when he forgets."

"Softly! What dost thou know of softness, old Ironfeet?" Bagheera grunted "His face is all bruised today by thy—softness. *Ugh.*"

"Better he should be bruised from head to foot by me who love him than that he should come to harm through ignorance," Baloo answered very earnestly. "I am now teaching him the Master Words of the jungle that shall protect him with the birds and the Snake-People, and all that hunt on four feet, except his own pack. He can now claim protection, if he will only remember the words, from all in the jungle. Is not that worth a little beating?"

"Well, look to it then that thou dost not kill the man-cub. He is no tree-trunk to sharpen thy blunt claws upon. But what are those Master Words? I am more

likely to give help than to ask it"—Bagheera stretched out one paw and admired the steel-blue, ripping-chisel talons at the end of it—"still I should like to know."

"I will call Mowgli and he shall say them—if he will. Come, Little Brother!"

"My head is ringing like a bee-tree," said a sullen little voice over their heads, and Mowgli slid down a tree-trunk very angry and indignant, adding as he reached the ground: "I come for Bagheera and not for thee, fat old Baloo!"

"That is all one to me," said Baloo, though he was hurt and grieved. "Tell Bagheera, then, the Master Words of the jungle that I have taught thee this day."

"Master Words for which people?" said

Mowgli, delighted to show off. "The jungle has many tongues. *I* know them all."

"A little thou knowest, but not much. See, O Bagheera, they never thank their teacher. Not one small wolfing has ever come back to thank old Baloo for his teachings. Say the word for the Hunting-People then—great scholar."

"We be of one blood, ye and I," said Mowgli, giving the words the bear accent which all the Hunting-People use.

"Good. Now for the birds."

Mowgli repeated, with the kite's whistle at the end of the sentence.

"Now for the Snake-People," said Bagheera.

The answer was a perfectly indescribable hiss, and Mowgli kicked up his feet behind, clapped his hands together to applaud himself, and jumped on to Bagheera's back, where he sat sideways, drumming with his heels on the glossy skin and making the worst faces he could think of at Baloo.

"There—there! That was worth a little bruise," said the brown bear tenderly. "Some day thou wilt remember me." Then he turned aside to tell Bagheera how he had begged the Master Words from Hathi the Wild Elephant, who knows all about these things, and how Hathi had taken Mowgli down to a pool to get the Snake Word from a water-snake, because Baloo could not pronounce it, and how Mowgli was now reasonably safe against all accidents in the jungle, because neither snake, bird, nor beast would hurt him.

A Fairy Tale Verse

Miss Goldilocks, out walking, spied
The Three Bears' house and went inside.
She sipped some supper from each cup,
And ate the wee bear's porridge up.
Three easy chairs she found to try,
But one was hard and one too high;
'Twas baby bear's she liked the best.
Then wishing for a bit of rest

Goldilocks

She sampled all the beds upstairs
And went to sleep in a baby bear's.
But when she woke, and by the bed
Saw all the bears, she quickly fled.

38

S.O.S. & Other Emergency Breakfasts

Grandfathers can lure even the sleepiest grandkids out of bed with the delicious smells of fried potatoes, eggs, or hotcakes. Even if the bread has gone stale, you can still make the best French toast. No time for pancakes? Just whip them up in the blender. Can't sit for a hot meal? Wrap it in a tortilla and make it instantly portable for a meal on the go. Try these family favorites with your grandchildren and shoo away the morning groggies in your household.

Rais'n Shine French Toast

3 eggs
4 tablespoons milk
1/4 teaspoon vanilla
1 tablespoon cinnamon
2 tablespoons sugar
Butter or oil for frying
8 slices raisin (or other) bread
Powdered sugar or maple syrup

1. Mix eggs, milk, vanilla, cinnamon, and sugar thoroughly in a shallow bowl.
2. Heat oil or butter in skillet or griddle on medium-high heat.
3. Dip each slice of bread in egg batter until covered, but do not soak.
4. Fry bread slices until brown crust forms on both sides.
5. Serve immediately, topped with butter and powdered sugar or maple syrup.

Makes 4 servings

S.O.S. ("Stuff" on a Shingle)

1/2 pound lean ground beef
1 cup evaporated milk
2 tablespoons butter
Salt and pepper to taste
1 cup water
4 tablespoons flour
6 slices toast

1. Brown ground beef in hot fry pan until cooked through. Drain fat.
2. Stir in milk, butter, salt and pepper, and 1/2 cup water. Bring to a simmer.
3. Meanwhile, mix remaining water with flour. Slowly stir into simmering beef. Remove from heat when mixture has thickened.
4. Spoon mixture over toast and serve hot.

Makes 3 servings

Apple Hotcakes

1 egg
1 tablespoon sugar
1 tablespoon softened butter
1 apple, peeled, cored, and sliced
1 cup evaporated milk or buttermilk
1 cup pancake or biscuit mix
Oil or butter for frying
Maple syrup or apple butter

1. In blender, mix egg, sugar, butter, apple, and milk until smooth.
2. Add pancake or biscuit mix and blend.
3. Heat oil or butter in skillet or griddle over medium heat.
4. Drop batter by tablespoonfuls and fry until bubbles appear on top and edges become crisp. Flip once and heat through.
5. Serve warm with maple syrup or apple butter.

Makes 4 servings

B'fast Burritos

1 tablespoon butter
1 potato, quartered and sliced
1/2 onion, chopped
4 beaten eggs
4 ounces turkey or other favorite pre-cooked sausage, sliced
4 ounces grated cheddar cheese
4 whole-wheat tortillas
Hot pepper sauce to taste

1. Melt butter in fry pan over medium-high heat. Fry potatoes and onion, turning frequently, until brown and cooked through.
2. Stir in beaten eggs and turkey sausage. Heat until eggs are at desirable consistency.
3. Sprinkle grated cheese on top and allow it to melt.
4. Place a serving of scrambled mixture in the center of each tortilla. Add pepper sauce to taste, and then wrap with tortilla and serve.
5. If you're making these to go, wrap each burrito in aluminum foil to keep warm.

Makes 4 servings

3

Chicken Little

Once upon a time, there was a sweet, small chicken named Chicken Little. One morning as she was scratching the ground in her yard, looking for a juicy worm or two, a pebble fell off the roof of her house and hit her right on the head.

"Oh dear!" she cried. "The sky is falling! I must go and tell the king!" And with that, she set off for the palace at once.

A little way down the road, Chicken Little met Henny Penny, who was doing her grocery shopping. "Where are you going?" asked Henny Penny.

"I'm going to tell the king that the sky is falling! A piece of it fell and hit me on the head this very day!" Chicken Little answered.

"May I go with you?" begged Henny Penny, and Chicken Little agreed.

As they traveled down the road, they saw Cocky Locky, who was just about to go to the post office.

"Say, where are you two going in such a rush?" he asked.

"We're going to tell the king that the sky is falling!" Henny Penny said.

"How do you know it's falling?"

"Because Chicken Little told me so!" said Henny Penny with annoyance.

"A piece of it fell on my head!" declared Chicken Little.

Forgetting his letters, Cocky Locky asked, "May I go with you?"

"Certainly," Chicken Little and Henny Penny answered, and the three were off.

They had just turned a corner when they almost ran into Goosey Loosey, who had decided to go to the movies that afternoon.

"Watch where you're going!" she spluttered. "What's the matter with you three?"

Cocky Locky answered, "We have to hurry and tell the king that the sky is falling!"

Chicken Little

"The sky is falling?" Goosey Loosey asked with wide eyes, "How do you know that?"

"Henny Penny told me," said Cocky Locky.

"Chicken Little told me," said Henny Penny.

"A piece of it fell and hit me on the head!" cried Chicken Little.

"I didn't realize how serious this was!" said Goosey Loosey. "May I join you?"

"Of course!" they exclaimed. Then Goosey Loosey followed Chicken Little, Henny Penny, and Cocky Locky down the road. After walking for some time, they decided to take a short rest. Suddenly, Foxy Loxy slipped out from behind some rocks. All of the birds looked very tasty to him, and he asked, with a sly smile, "Where are you all off to on this fine afternoon?"

"The sky is falling and we are going to tell the king!" they answered.

"But how do you know that?" Foxy Loxy inquired.

"Cocky Locky told me," declared Goosey Loosey.

"Henny Penny told me," answered Cocky Locky.

"Chicken Little told me," provided Henny Penny.

"And a piece of it fell and almost squashed me!" finished Chicken Little. "So, now we must go and tell the king!"

"But you silly birds have been going the wrong way!" Foxy Loxy told them. "Let me show you the correct way to the palace."

"Of course!" said the birds, and they followed Foxy Loxy all the way

Chicken Little

to a dark hole in the side of a hill.

Foxy Loxy motioned them in. "Just step through here. The palace is just through this tunnel, on the other side of the hill!"

Now, luckily for the foolish birds, a sharp-eyed squirrel had seen the whole thing, and before even one could set a wing in, she called to them, "Don't go in! Don't go in! All your necks he'll wring, and you'll never see the king!"

The birds turned to run, and Foxy Loxy sprang forward and almost got ahold of Goosey Loosey. But the little squirrel threw a stone and got him—BONK!—right on the forehead.

Foxy Loxy rubbed his head. "The sky *is* falling!" he screamed, and dove into the hole.

Happy to escape from the wicked fox, Chicken Little, Henny Penny, Cocky Locky, and Goosey Loosey all ran as fast as they could for the palace.

Finally, they arrived at the gate and were admitted inside. They were brought before the throne of the wise king, and all at once they shouted: "The sky is falling! The sky is falling!"

"How do you know the sky is falling?" asked the king.

"Because a piece of it fell on my head," said Chicken Little.

"Come a little closer, Chicken Little," said the king. He leaned forward and plucked a pebble from the feathers on Chicken Little's head.

"Look, it wasn't the sky at all! It was just a little pebble that fell on you!" The king chuckled. "Now, you should all go home in peace. Maybe next time you won't be so quick to jump to conclusions."

So, the silly birds left the palace and started on the long walk back home, weary, but a little bit wiser. ✦

The Frogs & The Well

Three frogs lived happily in a nice wet marsh. It got very hot one summer and the marsh dried up. The frogs had to look for a new home because frogs like nice damp places. They hopped and hopped around and soon came to a deep well. They took one great big leap to the side of the well and looked down. One frog said to the others, "This looks good. A nice dark well! Let us jump in!" But another, who was the wisest, said, "Wait just a minute! What if this well is dried up like the marsh? How will we get out if so? Let's keep searching."

Moral: Think before you act and look before you leap!

As I Grew Older

BY LANGSTON HUGHES

It was a long time ago.
I have almost forgotten my dream.
But it was there then,
In front of me,
Bright like a sun—
My dream.
And then the wall rose,
Rose slowly,
Slowly,
Between me and my dream.
Rose until it touched the sky—
The wall.
Shadow.
I am black.
I lie down in the shadow.

No longer the light of my dream
    before me,
Above me.
Only the thick wall.
Only the shadow.
My hands!
My dark hands!
Break through the wall!
Find my dream!
Help me to shatter this darkness,
To smash this night,
To break this shadow
Into a thousand lights of sun,
Into a thousand whirling dreams
of sun!

LEGENDARY TALL TALES: HOW DAVY CROCKETT BECAME A CONGRESSMAN

many, many stories are told about the great frontiersman and hunter, Davy Crockett—most told by the man himself! Davy boasted that he was half-horse, half-alligator, with just a touch of snapping turtle. Legends say that he single-handedly tamed a panther and that he caused a raccoon to fall out of a tree just by outsmiling it.

Davy Crockett seemed bigger than life. And although he is well known for his outdoor adventures, did you know that he was also a congressman? It's hard to believe this rough-and-tumble man was a representative in Washington, D.C., but he was. He supported Native-American rights to land and wanted farmers to have more say in the government. But Davy Crockett had to fight to become a congressman too, and here is one legend of how he did it.

One day, Davy traveled to a town to give a speech and gather votes for himself. He showed up late (on account of a cougar he had to battle along the way!) and found that his opponent was already giving a very long speech.

"Now no one's going to listen to what I have to say," thought Davy. And it was true—once his opponent's long, boring speech was over, people began to drift away. Until Davy Crockett got up and declared that the debates should be moved to the local restaurant and saloon, where meals and drinks would be on him! Everyone cheered and charged into the establishment. Soon, everyone was having a grand old time, eating and drinking, all thanks to Mr. Davy Crockett!

But when the bill showed up, Davy

was amazed to see how much everything cost. He told Brown, the owner, "I wasn't quite expecting such a large crowd to turn out. Why don't you keep this on record and I'll come back tomorrow and pay you everything I owe?"

Brown told Davy he'd have to pay; otherwise he would throw Davy in jail. Davy thought he'd be in big trouble, but then he remembered an old bearskin he had with him and decided to offer it up as payment. He gave it to Brown, and the bill was settled.

So Davy again went to the center of the village and began making a speech. But it had taken him so long to settle the matter of the bill that everyone was bored and hungry again. They called for another meal, and Davy of course obliged, amid many cheers of "Hurray for Davy Crockett!"

This time, Davy *knew* the owner would not be happy with him. And to make matters worse, he had no more bearskins to trade. He was just about to give up and head over to the jail, when he saw that Brown had folded the bearskin up and left it carelessly hanging off the end of the counter. Quick as a wink, Davy snatched it up. He did it so fast that no one noticed him take it.

"I hope you won't mind another bearskin as payment?" he asked Brown, as he handed over the bearskin again.

Davy could not believe it. And what was even more unbelievable was that the trick worked two more times! Each time the group would crowd into the restaurant and eat and drink to their hearts' delight, then Davy would pinch the bearskin and pay again. He paid for four different meals with the same skin. And he knew the people who had heard him that day would be sure to vote for him. And so, with a little help from a bearskin, Davy Crockett became a congressman. ⚘

Don't Lose Your Beans!

There are no age limits required for Mancala (considered the world's oldest game) which is why old and young alike can enjoy playing together. Each player tries to figure out how—by moving beans around the game board—to end up with more beans in their store than their opponent. Introduce your grandchildren to a basic version of this generational favorite by constructing the playing board and then testing your strategy against one another time and time again.

Bottom of an empty dozen-egg carton, two cups, 36 dried beans (or pebbles or marbles)

1. Position the egg carton between the two players with the long sides facing them. Place a cup at each end of the carton.

2. Place three beans in each of the egg carton depressions, or "pots." Leave the end cups, or "stores," empty. Each player claims the cup to the right as their "store," and owns the row of six "pots" in front of them.

3. Flip a coin to determine who goes first.

4. The first player removes all the beans from one of their pots. Then, starting with the pot to the left of the one emptied, the player drops, or "sows," one bean in each adjacent consecutive pot—including both stores and the opponent's pots—in a counterclockwise direction around the board. If the last bean lands in their own store, the player takes another turn. Otherwise, the play passes to the other player.

5. The game continues with each player taking turns sowing beans around the board.

The game ends when one player has no more beans in their pots. The player with the most beans in their store wins.

GAME VARIATION:

1. Flip a coin to determine who goes first.

2. Players take turns sowing beans in each pot counterclockwise around the board, including their own store but skipping their opponent's store. If the last bean a player sows lands in their own store, the player gets another turn. If the last bean a player sows ends up in an empty pot on their side, then that player captures all the beans from the opponent's pot directly opposite and puts them in their store.

3. The game continues until one player has cleared all the beans from the pots on their side of the board. If, in the next turn, the opponent can sow beans onto the empty side of the board, the play continues. If not, the remaining beans go into the player's store. The player with the most beans in their store wins.

Did you ever?

Grandfather Wisdoms

Genius is one percent inspiration and
ninety-nine percent perspiration.

—Thomas Edison

Experience is the mother of wisdom.
First think, and then speak.

Wise men talk because they have something to say;
fools, because they have to say something.

—Plato

It is not enough to have a good mind.
The main thing is to use it well.

—Rene Descartes

Ignorance is a cure for nothing.

—W.E.B. Du Bois

A man may die, nations may rise and fall, but an idea lives on. Ideas have endurance without death.

—JOHN F. KENNEDY

The most important part of the body is the brain.

—FRIDA KAHLO

Teachers open the door, but you must enter by yourself.

—CHINESE PROVERB

In a world that is changing all the time, no one's education is ever complete.

—MARGARET MEAD

THE WONDERFUL WIZARD OF OZ

by L. Frank Baum

"I think you are a very bad man," said Dorothy.

"Oh, no, my dear; I'm really a very good man; but I'm a very bad Wizard, I must admit."

"Can't you give me brains?" asked the Scarecrow.

"You don't need them. You are learning something every day. A baby has brains, but it doesn't know much. Experience is the only thing that brings knowledge, and the longer you are on earth the more experience you are sure to get."

"That may all be true," said the Scarecrow, "but I shall be very unhappy unless you give me brains."

The false wizard looked at him carefully.

"Well," he said, with a sigh, "I'm not much of a magician, as I said; but if you will come to me tomorrow morning, I will stuff your head with brains. I cannot tell you how to use them, however; you must find that out for yourself."

"Oh, thank you—thank you!" cried the Scarecrow. "I'll find a way to use them, never fear!"

"But how about my courage?" asked the Lion, anxiously.

"You have plenty of courage, I am sure," answered Oz. "All you need is confidence in yourself. There is no living thing that is not afraid when it faces danger. True courage is in facing danger when you are afraid, and that kind of courage you have in plenty."

"Perhaps I have, but I'm scared just the same," said the Lion. "I shall really be very unhappy unless you give me the sort of courage that makes one forget he is afraid."

"Very well; I will give you that sort of courage tomorrow," replied Oz.

"How about my heart?" asked the Tin Woodman.

"Why, as for that," answered Oz, "I think you are wrong to want a heart. It makes most people unhappy. If you only knew it, you are in luck not to have a heart."

"That must be a matter of opinion," said the Tin Woodman. "For my part, I will bear all the unhappiness without a murmur, if you will give me the heart."

"Very well," answered Oz, meekly. "Come to me tomorrow and you shall have a heart. I have played Wizard for so many years that I may as well continue the part a little longer."

Next morning the Scarecrow said to his friends:

"Congratulate me. I am going to Oz to get my brains at last. When I return I shall be as other men are."

"I have always liked you as you were," said Dorothy, simply.

"It is kind of you to like a Scarecrow," he replied. "But surely you will think more of me when you hear the splendid thoughts my new brain is going to turn out." Then he said good-bye to them all in a cheerful voice and went to the Throne Room, where he rapped upon the door.

"Come in," said Oz.

The Scarecrow went in and found the little man sitting down by the window, engaged in deep thought.

"I have come for my brains," remarked the Scarecrow, a little uneasily.

"Oh, yes; sit down in that chair, please," replied Oz. "You must excuse me for taking you head off, but I shall have to do it in order to put your brains in their proper place."

"That's all right," said the Scarecrow. "You are quite welcome to take my head off, as long as it will be a better one when you put it on again."

So the Wizard unfastened his head and emptied out the straw. Then he entered the back room and took up a measure of bran, which he mixed with a great many pins and needles. Having shaken them together thoroughly, he filled the top of the Scarecrow's head with the mixture and stuffed the rest of the space with straw, to hold it in place. When he had fastened the Scarecrow's head on his body again he said to him,

"Hereafter you will be a great man, for I have given you a lot of bran-new brains."

The Scarecrow was both pleased and proud at the fulfillment of his greatest wish, and having thanked Oz warmly he went back to his friends.

Dorothy looked at him curiously. He head was quite bulging out at the top with brains.

"How do you feel?" she asked.

"I feel wise, indeed," he answered, earnestly. "When I get used to my brains I shall know everything."

"Why are those needles and pins sticking out of your head?" asked the Tin Woodman.

"That is proof that he is sharp," remarked the Lion.

"Well, I must go to Oz and get my heart," said the Woodman. So he walked to the Throne Room and knocked at the door.

"Come in," called Oz, and the Woodman entered and said,

"I have come for my heart."

"Very well," answered the little man. "But I shall have to cut a hole in your breast, so I can put your heart in the right place. I hope it won't hurt you."

"Oh, no;" answered the Woodman. "I shall not feel it at all."

So Oz brought a pair of tinners' shears and cut a small, square hole in the left side of the Tin Woodman's breast. Then, going to a chest of drawers, he took out a pretty heart, made entirely of silk and stuffed with sawdust.

"Isn't it a beauty?" he asked.

"It is, indeed!" replied the Woodman, who was greatly pleased. "But is it a kind heart?"

"Oh, very!" answered Oz. He put the heart in the Woodman's breast and then replaced the square of tin, soldering it neatly together where it had been cut.

"There," said he; "now you have a heart that any man might be proud of. I'm sorry I had to put a patch on your breast, but it really couldn't be helped."

"Never mind the patch," exclaimed the happy Woodman. "I am very grateful to you, and shall never forget your kindness."

"Don't speak of it," replied Oz.

Then the Tin Woodman went back to his friends, who wished him every joy on account of his good fortune.

The Lion now walked to the Throne Room and knocked at the door.

"Come in," said Oz.

"I have come for my courage," announced the Lion, entering the room.

"Very well," answered the little man; "I will get it for you."

He went to a cupboard and reaching up to a high shelf took down a square green bottle, the contents of which he poured into a green-gold dish, beautifully carved. Placing this before the Cowardly Lion, who sniffed at it as if he did not like it, the Wizard said,

"Drink."

"What is it?" asked the Lion.

"Well," answered Oz, "if it were inside of you, it would be courage. You know, of course, that courage is always inside one; so that this really cannot be called courage until you have swallowed it. Therefore I advise you to drink it as soon as possible."

The Lion hesitated no longer, but drank till the dish was empty.

"How do you feel now?" asked Oz.

"Full of courage," replied the Lion, who went joyfully back to his friends to tell them of his good fortune.

Oz, left to himself, smiled to think of his success in giving the Scarecrow and the Tin Woodman and the Lion exactly what they thought they wanted. 🧚

I would be true, for there are
those who trust me,

I would be pure, for there are
those who care,

I would be strong, for there
is much to suffer,

I would be brave, for there is
much to dare,

I would be a friend of all, the
foe, the friendless,

I would be giving and forget
the gift,

I would be humble, for I
know my weakness,

I would look up, and laugh
and love and live.

—ANONYMOUS

Psychic Parlor Amusements

It's always good to have some parlor tricks up your sleeve for instant entertainment and a few laughs. Try these tricks on your grandchildren before teaching them the secrets. Then the next time you want to amuse friends and family members, offer to play the role of assistant and watch your grandchildren have fun showing off their special "extrasensory" abilities.

TRICKY DICE
Large clear glass of water, three acrylic dice

Start by asking a volunteer to drop three dice into the water. Ask them to hold the glass above their head and, without letting anyone else sneak a peek, look at the numbers on the bottoms of the dice and add them together in their head. When your volunteer places the glass back on the table, dip your finger into the water and touch your forehead. Close your eyes and concentrate deeply, then announce the total. Watch your volunteer's face light up when you say the right answer.

THE SECRET: When you dip your finger into the water, take a quick glance at the tops of the dice. Add the totals in your head while you're "concentrating," then subtract that number from 21. (The tops and bottoms of dice always total seven, so you can do this trick with as many dice as you want; simply multiply the number of dice you use by seven to know the number you need to subtract the total from.)

MIND-READING MAGIC DECK OF CARDS

This trick works best when you have a ready audience of friends or family members. Ask for a volunteer from the group to stand and face the others while holding a deck of cards facedown behind their back. Blindfold your volunteer and ask them to pick a card from the middle of the deck, and then have them hold the card with its face touching their forehead and its back facing the audience. At this time, instruct your audience to focus on the drawn card and concentrate deeply until a particular image comes to mind. Tell them that in a group, the powers of ESP can be very strong, and the chances of being able to "read" the mystery card can be greatly improved. Then, ask your volunteer to slip the drawn card into his back pocket.

Take back the remaining deck of cards and remove the blindfold. Ask your volunteer to pick anyone in the audience to guess the mystery card. That person names the card, and when the volunteer pulls the card out of his back pocket, it is the very same card the audience member named.

THE SECRET: Before you begin the trick, flip the top and bottom cards of the deck. Your volunteer will think they are holding the deck upside down. When the volunteer pull a card from the pack and touches it to their forehead, they'll think the back of the card is facing the audience—but in reality, they're revealing the face of the card to the entire crowd.

A Fairy Tale Verse

Jack's the widow's boy who sold
Her cow for beans instead of gold;
The beans grew up to very high
That Jack one day climbed to the sky
And found the wicked giant's lair
(With only Mrs. Giant there);
He took the magic hen away
And called again the second day.

Jack and the Beanstalk

But on the third, the giant grim
In rage descended after him,
Jack quickly chopped the beanstalk down
And thus the giant broke his crown!

72

The Story of Blue Wings

By Mary Stewart

There was once an old apple orchard. It was full of beautiful things, particularly in the springtime. Then the trees were covered with pink and white blossoms and the soft green grass was sprinkled with dandelions.

But there was something in the orchard more beautiful than blossoms and grass and dandelions. Sometimes there was a flash of blue wings above the trees. Then a bird's song rang out sweet and clear. It came from the owner of those splendid blue wings and you knew that the king of the orchard had returned from his winter's trip. The bluebird had come home.

High up in an old tree there was a little hole and there the bluebird made his nest. From the outside the hole looked dark and hard; but inside it was as soft and cozy as the prettiest nest in the world. There lived the mother and father bluebird with their five little baby birds.

During the summer the young ones learned to fly. They learned, too, a few notes of the beautiful songs they were to sing. Their mother told them that when the cold weather came they would fly to the warm South. Then in the spring they would come back to the orchard with wings that would flash and with songs that would be like the first happy call of spring.

When the first cold weather came four of the young birds flew away with their father and mother. But one was left behind. Poor little bird! He had fallen from a tree and one wing was broken. He could not fly. He lay on the ground, his blue feathers dull and his eyes dim.

There a little girl found him one morning. She lifted him carefully and carried him to the white farmhouse. She laid the poor little

The Story of Blue Wings

creature in a big wooden cage and fed him with bread crumbs soaked in water.

In a little while his eyes grew bright and he tried to fly a little. When he found that he could not he gave a chirp of pain.

But soon with the little girl's care he grew strong again, and he and his little friend had happy times together even if he couldn't fly. The door of the cage was always open and Blue Wings, that is the name she gave him, would hop down to the table, and around the room, always ending his play by alighting upon the little girl's shoulder. He would eat from her hand. Sometimes he gave little chirps as if to say, "Thank you."

As the winter passed and the days grew warm and bright, Blue Wings longed more and more to fly among the trees. One day the window next to his cage was left wide open. Suddenly Blue Wings felt as if he must fly or his heart would break. And then he lifted his wings! He flew right out of the window! Through the orchard he darted above the trees, his blue wings flashing in the sunshine.

As he flew higher and higher he sang a song clearer and sweeter than he had ever sung before. The little girl heard it as she stood at her door, smiling up into the blue sky. Blue Wings never came back to the cage, or to the farmhouse kitchen. But whenever the little girl saw a wonderfully beautiful blue flash through the branches or heard a beautiful bird's song, she knew that Blue Wings was near.

ACTIVITIES

Birds of a Feather

*S*pending time observing nature is a wonderful way to share discoveries with your grandchildren. Bird-watching is more than simply looking for and identifying birds: It's learning how to listen for specific songs, calls, and other noises, such as tapping or drumming. Plan your excursion and take along binoculars, a tape recorder, and a sketch pad to take descriptive notes or draw pictures of the birds you see.

Most bird-watchers learn to identify birds by their vocalizations, which tend to be specific to a species; however, some birds mimic other sounds. Catbirds, or mockingbirds, for example, copy the songs of other songbirds, and starlings will mimic car alarms and even human voices!

Here are some sounds to listen for:
- Certain water birds, such as geese, ducks, and swans, are identifiable by honks, quacks, and hoots.
- Sparrows and warblers repeat the same note quickly so that it sounds like a trill, a twitter, or a churr.

- Woodpeckers make rhythmical tapping or drumming sounds while looking for insects in tree bark.
- Grouse and prairie chickens make drumming and booming noises to attract mates.

Whether on a walk in the country, a nature preserve, or through an urban neighborhood, be on the lookout for abandoned or empty nests such as these:

- Along rocky beaches and shellbars, look for shallow, scratched-out depressions in the ground or leaves, called **SCRAPES**. Such nests are common among certain coastal birds, such as the red-billed black or American oystercatcher.

- Look for elevated **PLATFORM** nests in treetops or in areas of shallow water. Hawks, cormorants, eagles, herons, and ospreys build these flat, slightly depressed nests to keep their eggs out of the reach of predators.
- Most songbirds build **CUPPED** nests, which are round and solidly built. These are complex bird nests designed to keep eggs warm and protected.
- **ADHERENT** nests are plastered under the eves of buildings, along stone ledges, or barn walls. If you spot such a cup-shaped nest built of mud, chances are you're looking at the home of a barn swallow.
- Vireos build **PENSILE** nests, cup-shaped structures that hang from tree branches by their stiffly woven rims.
- If you see a cup-shaped nest that looks like a small bag swinging freely from a tree branch, you've probably found a **PENDULOUS** nest built by an oriole.

...Flock Together

You may know that a group of birds is called a **FLOCK**, but did you know that a group of chickens is called a **PEEP**, or that a group of hummingbirds is called a **TROUBLING**? Here words for some other flocks:

A **FLIGHT** of cormorants ■ A **MURDER** of crows ■ A **DULE** of doves ■ A **PADDLING** of ducks ■ A **CONVOCATION** of eagles ■ A **CHARM** of finches ■ A **GAGGLE** of geese ■ A **COLONY** of gulls ■ A **BROOD** of hens ■ A **BAND** of jays ■ A **CONCENTRATION** of kingfishers ■ An **EXALTATION** of larks ■ A **RAFT** of loons ■ A **TIDING** of magpies ■ A **WISDOM** of owls ■ A **COMPANY** of parrots ■ A **COVEY** of quail ■ A **CONSPIRACY** of ravens ■ A **PARLIAMENT** of rooks ■ A **QUARREL** of sparrows ■ A **MURMURATION** of starlings ■ A **BALLET** of swans

Caterpillar

BY CHRISTINA ROSSETTI

Brown and furry
Caterpillar in a hurry,
Take your walk
To the shady leaf, or stalk,
Or what not,
Which may be the chosen spot.
No toad spy you,
Hovering bird of prey pass by you;
Spin and die,
To live again a butterfly.

ALICE'S ADVENTURES IN WONDERLAND

by Lewis Carroll

The Caterpillar and Alice looked at each other for some time in silence: at last the Caterpillar took the hookah out of its mouth, and addressed her in a languid, sleepy voice.

"Who are *you*?" said the Caterpillar.

This was not an encouraging opening for a conversation. Alice replied, rather shyly, "I—I hardly know, Sir, just at present—at least I know who I *was* when I got up this morning, but I think I must have been changed several times since then."

"What do you mean by that?" said the Caterpillar, sternly. "Explain yourself!"

"I can't explain *myself*, I'm afraid, Sir," said Alice, "because I'm not myself, you see."

"I don't see," said the Caterpillar.

"I'm afraid I can't put it more clearly," Alice

replied, very politely, "for I can't understand it myself, to begin with; and being so many different sizes in a day is very confusing."

"It isn't," said the Caterpillar.

"Well, perhaps you haven't found it so yet," said Alice; "but when you have to turn into a chrysalis—you will some day, you know—and then after that into a butterfly, I should think you'll feel a little queer, won't you!"

"Not a bit," said the Caterpillar.

"Well, perhaps *your* feelings may be different," said Alice: "all I know is, it would feel very queer to *me*."

"You!" said the Caterpillar contemptuously. "Who are *you*?"

Which brought them back again to the beginning of the conversation. Alice felt a little irritated at the Caterpillar's making such *very* short remarks, and she drew herself up and said, very gravely, "I think you ought to tell me who *you* are, first."

"Why?" said the Caterpillar.

Here was another puzzling question; and, as Alice could not think of any good reason, and the Caterpillar seemed to be in a *very* unpleasant state of mind, she turned away.

"Come back!" the Caterpillar called after her. "I've something important to say!"

This sounded promising, certainly. Alice turned and came back again.

"Keep your temper," said the Caterpillar.

"Is that all?" said Alice, swallowing down her anger as well as she could.

"No," said the Caterpillar.

Alice thought she might as well wait, as she had nothing else to do, and perhaps after all it might tell her something worth hearing. For some minutes it puffed away without speaking; but at last it unfolded its arms, took the hookah out of its mouth again, and said, "So you think you're changed, do you?"

"I'm afraid I am, Sir," said Alice. "I can't remember things as I used—and I don't keep the same size for ten minutes together!"

"Can't remember *what* things?" said the Caterpillar.

"Well, I've tried to say *'How doth the little busy bee,'* but it all came different!" Alice replied in a very melancholy voice.

"Repeat *'You are old, Father William,'*" said the Caterpillar.

Alice folded her hands, and began:

> *"You are old, Father William," the young man said*
> *"And your hair has become very white,*
> *And yet you incessantly stand on your head—*
> *Do you think, at your age, it is right?"*
>
> *"In my youth," Father William replied to his son,*
> *"I feared it might injure the brain;*

But, now that I'm perfectly sure I have none,
Why, I do it again and again."

"You are old," said the youth, "as I mentioned before
And have grown most uncommonly fat,
Yet you turned a back-somersault in at the door
Pray, what is the reason of that?"

"In my youth," said the sage, as he shook his grey locks,
"I kept all my limbs very supple
By the use of this ointment—one shilling the box—
Allow me to sell you a couple?"

"You are old," said the youth, "and your jaws are too weak
For anything tougher than suet;
Yet you finished the goose, with the bones and the beak—
Pray, how did you manage to do it?"

"In my youth," said his father, "I took to the law,
And argued each case with my wife;
And the muscular strength, which it gave to my jaw
Has lasted the rest of my life."

"You are old," said the youth, "one would hardly suppose
That your eye was as steady as ever;
Yet you balanced an eel on the end of your nose—
What made you so awfully clever?"

"I have answered three questions, and that is enough,"
Said his father, "Don't give yourself airs!
Do you think I can listen all day to such stuff?
Be off, or I'll kick you down-stairs!"

That is not said right," said the Caterpillar.

Not *quite* right, I'm afraid," said Alice, timidly: "some of the words have got altered."

"It is wrong from beginning to end," said the Caterpillar, decidedly; and there was silence for some minutes.

The Caterpillar was the first to speak.

"What size do you want to be?" it asked.

"Oh, I'm not particular as to size," Alice hastily replied: "only one doesn't like changing so often, you know."

"I *don't* know," said the Caterpillar.

Alice said nothing: she had never been so much contradicted in all her life before, and she felt that she was losing her temper.

"Are you content now!" said the Caterpillar.

"Well, I should like to be a *little* larger, Sir, if you wouldn't mind," said Alice: "three inches is such a wretched height to be."

"It is a very good height indeed!" said the Caterpillar angrily, rearing itself upright as it spoke (it was exactly three inches high).

"But I'm not used to it!" pleaded poor Alice in a piteous tone. And she thought to herself, "I wish the creatures wouldn't be so easily offended!"

"You'll get used to it in time," said the Caterpillar; and it put the hookah into its mouth, and began smoking again.

This time Alice waited patiently until it chose to speak again. In a minute or two the Caterpillar took the hookah out of its mouth, and yawned once or twice, and shook itself. Then it got down off the mushroom, and crawled away into the grass, merely remarking, as it went, "One side will make you grow taller, and the other side will make you grow shorter."

"One side of *what*? The other side of *what*?" thought Alice to herself.

"Of the mushroom," said the Caterpillar, just as if she had asked it aloud; and in another moment it was out of sight.

Alice remained looking thoughtfully at the mushroom for a minute, trying to make out which were the two sides of it; and, as it was perfectly round, she found this a very difficult question. However, at last she stretched her arms round it as far as they would go, and broke off a bit of the edge with each hand.

"And now which is which?" she said to herself, and nibbled a little of the right-hand bit to try the effect. The next moment she felt a violent blow underneath her chin: it had struck her foot!

She was a good deal frightened by this very sudden change, but she felt that there was no time to be lost, as she was shrinking rapidly: so she set to work at once to eat some of the other bit. Her chin was pressed so closely against her foot, that there was hardly room to open her mouth; but she did it at last, and managed to swallow a morsel of the left-hand bit.

A Fairy Tale Verse

Quaint Alice trailed the rabbit, dressed
So strangely in a coat and vest
And at the bottom of the hole,
Had many more adventures droll;
By tasting "Drink Me" she grew smaller,
By sipping something else, was taller;
She met the Duchess, Cheshire Cat,
The Mad March Hare and folk like that,

Alice in Wonderland

She stirred her tea and played croquet,
In court had nothing right to say,
And when it all began to seem
Mixed up, discovered 'twas a dream.

When I was young I used to wait
On master and hand him his plate
Pass him the bottle when he got dry
And brush away the blue-tail fly

Chorus
Jimmy crack corn, and I don't care
Jimmy crack corn, and I don't care
Jimmy crack corn, and I don't care
My master's gone away

When he would ride in the afternoon
I'd follow him with my hickory broom
The pony being rather shy
When bitten by the blue-tail fly

Chorus

One day he rode around the farm
Flies so numerous that they did swarm

Blue Tail Fly
(Jimmy Crack Corn)

One chanced to bite him on the thigh
The devil take the blue-tail fly

Chorus

Well the pony jumped, he start, he pitch
He threw my master in the ditch
He died and the jury wondered why
The verdict was the blue-tail fly

Chorus

Now he lies beneath the 'simmons tree
His epitaph is there to see
"Beneath this stone I'm forced to lie
The victim of the blue-tail fly"

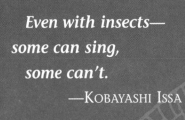

*Even with insects—
some can sing,
some can't.*
—KOBAYASHI ISSA

*A stem of grass,
Whereon in vain,
A dragon fly attempts
to light.*
—BASHO

The moon is clouded o'er,
And soon the moths will sally forth
To dance upon the moor.

—Joso

Climb Mount Fuji,
O snail,
But slowly, slowly.

—Kobayashi Issa

93

The Fly & The Moth

One night, a fly noticed an open jar of strawberry jam on a table. The jam looked so sweet and tasty that he immediately flew inside the jar to have a treat. Unfortunately, he became stuck in the sticky jam. As he was struggling to get out, a moth flew by and instead of helping him said, "It serves you right! Didn't you realize how thick and sticky that jam would be before you jumped into it?" A little while later, someone turned a lamp on in the room, and the moth, who could not resist the light, smacked into it again and again until he had a big headache. "What's this?" said the fly, who had managed to scramble out of the jar finally. "You scolded me for my sweet tooth, but you yourself are playing with fire!"

Moral: Do not criticize your friends' mistakes and ignore your own.

ACTIVITIES

Capture a Spider Web

Spider webs are fragile wonders of nature, as you and your grandchildren know if you've ever tried to touch one only to find the silk strands whisked away into the wind or nearby branches. If you happen upon an abandoned orb web or sheet web, here's a way to capture its beauty and intricate details without getting sticky fingers.

Black cardboard, spray glue or hair spray, small manicure scissors

The secret to success with this project is patience and gentleness. Some webs may be trickier than others to capture, so try to locate several spider webs in advance. That way, if one comes apart, your grandchild can try again. Start by cutting a black piece of cardboard a few inches larger in diameter than the spider web you want to collect. Spray one side of the cardboard lightly with glue or hair spray. Hold the sticky side up to the web, then slowly and gently press the cardboard against the web until all strands are touching it. Use the small manicure scissors to carefully detach the spider web from its support branches. Now you can carry the web away.

SPIDER HOMES

■ Not all spiders live in webs. Primitive ones, such as trapdoor spiders, baboon spiders, and tarantulas live in **SILK-LINED BURROWS** in the ground. Each year, as trapdoor spiders grow, they add another silk rim to their door. You can tell the age of the spider based on the number of rims.

- Garden spiders, such as the golden silk spider, the black-and-yellow garden spider, and the marbled spider, build spiral-shaped orb webs. You can find circular **ORB WEBS**, spun in rays and spirals of silk, in sunny places outdoors around buildings, gardens, and tall grasses.

- Grass spiders build **FUNNEL WEBS**. These weavers build horizontal sheet-like webs with a tornado-shaped funnel in the grass. These webs are most obvious in the morning when glistening with dew. The funnel serves as a hiding place for the spider as she awaits her prey.

- Small, dark, and shiny **SHEET WEB** spiders are nocturnal hunters that weave small, horizontal sheets of webbing that can be flat or dome-shaped. They're among the biggest spider families in the world and are found in all kinds of habitats.

- **COBWEB** spiders, such as the red-bellied black widow or the long-legged cellar spider, build irregular webs out of soft and fluffy silk both outdoors and indoors in protected places. These spiders tend to hang upside down in their webs.

- **TRIANGLE WEB** spiders spin three-sided, triangular webs. The spider waits for prey on one corner. When an insect lands on the web, the spider shakes it until the insect gets caught in the sticky silk.

Legendary Tall Tales: Sweet Betsy from Pike

during the Gold Rush of 1849, it seemed like the whole country had caught gold fever. Many pioneers loaded up their wagons, ready to brave terrible weather, sickness, and attacks by Native Americans and wild animals just for the chance to strike it rich in California.

The small community of Pike County, Missouri, was no different. Every day, more and more people were heading west. Betsy felt sad each time she saw more of her friends head off. Betsy was a spunky girl who desperately wanted to try her hand at gold panning and felt sure she'd be able to make a new life in California.

"Who knows what could be waiting for me in California?" she thought. "There's a whole world out there that's just begging to be explored."

Betsy tried to convince her parents to head west with the wagon trains, but they only laughed at her foolishness. Her father was a storekeeper and had a very successful business.

"Betsy, I *sell* my goods to those gold-hungry fools, I don't *join* them!" he told her.

But Betsy had her mind set for the golden land of California, and one day she got her chance to strike out.

Ike was a young man about Betsy's age who often helped Betsy's father in the store. One day, he didn't show up for work, and Betsy's father sent her to see what was keeping him. She found him loading up a small wagon with dry goods.

"And where are you off to? My father's pretty mad at you for not showing up this morning." Ike's yellow dog ran out and gave Betsy's hand a friendly lick.

Ike said, "I know that was wrong of me, but I'm setting off for California today. I can't let anything stop me."

"California, huh?" said Betsy. "And where'd you get these dry goods from?"

Ike turned bright red. "Well, your father was going to throw this stuff out anyway, so..."

Betsy saw her chance and jumped at it. "Listen, Ike, I don't want to tell my father about this, but the only way I'll keep quiet is if you take me to California with you."

Ike didn't want to take Betsy, but she fought so hard that he finally agreed to meet her that evening at midnight and set off.

Betsy was so excited to be heading to California that she barely felt sad at having to leave her home.

"It doesn't matter," she thought. "Soon I'll be so rich I'll be able to afford to send a message back home."

So Ike and Betsy set out, along with a pair of oxen, a spotted hog, a Shanghai rooster, and Ike's faithful yellow dog. For a while, things went very well for the two. Betsy had never had a chance to talk to Ike before, and she was amazed to hear his thoughts. He'd always been so quiet as he worked in her father's store.

Sleeping under the bright stars and breathing in the fresh prairie air of Nebraska, Betsy certainly thought this adventure was turning out very well.

She soon had cause to change her mind. The next day, a spoke on the wheel broke and they lost most of the day fixing it. A few days later, the rooster got sick, and they had to leave it behind.

"Not to worry," Betsy told Ike, "I'll make sure we wake up in the morning." She was trying to be optimistic, but things just seemed to get worse and worse. Next they tried to ford a river and most of their supplies were washed away. They were forced to eat the spotted hog. They trudged over the Sierra Mountains and both caught terrible colds. They couldn't take care of the cattle anymore, and were forced to leave them behind. They stumbled onward, only carrying the bare minimum of supplies on their backs.

"Betsy," Ike said as they made their way up another rocky slope, "I'm starting to think this might not have been such a good idea."

"Don't worry, Ike," Betsy answered. "It'll all be worth it when we reach California. I can almost see that gold now!"

But the worst was yet to come. Ike and Betsy reached the treacherous desert and almost gave up all hope. It stretched on for miles and miles and miles. It was so hot, images swam in front of Betsy. Her eyes burned with the glare and she was constantly rubbing sand out of them. They were running out of food and water, and even Ike's yellow dog ran away. "Can't say I blame him," Ike said sadly.

Just as they were about to give up entirely, the desert started to thin out. A few more miles, and they suddenly saw a small town on the horizon.

"Ike, we made it! We're in California!" Betsy cheered. They hugged and danced with joy. Then they started for the town. "Don't you see, Ike? Now I can finally begin my adventures!"

Ike looked so sad that Betsy stopped short. "You look like a fella that just lost his best horse. What's the matter?"

"Now that we're in California and you're ready to begin your adventures, I guess you won't have any need for a boy from back home like me," he said in a small voice.

Betsy was shocked. She'd been around Ike for so long, they'd shared so many experiences, she couldn't imagine her life without him. Suddenly, she realized how much Ike meant to her.

"Ike, the only adventures I want to have are with you by my side," she declared, and Ike thought his heart would burst in two.

Ike and Betsy got married that very week. Some said they found gold in the California hills, and some said that they ended up fighting when Ike got jealous of all the attention the miners gave Betsy. But one thing was clear: sweet Betsy from Pike was never at a loss for adventures ever again!

Did you ever hear tell of
Sweet Betsy from Pike,
Who crossed the wide prairies
With her husband, Ike,
With two yoke of cattle
And one spotted hog,
A tall shanghai rooster,
And an old yeller dog?

Sing toorali—oorali—oorali ay!
Sing toorali—oorali—oorali ay!

The alkali desert
Was burning and bare
And Ike cried in fear,
"We are lost, I declare!
My dear old Pike County,
I'll go back to you."
Said Betsy, "You'll go by yourself,
If you do."

Sweet Betsy from Pike

Sing toorali—oorali—oorali ay!
Sing toorali—oorali—oorali ay!

They swam the wide rivers
And crossed the tall peaks
They camped on the prairie
For weeks upon weeks.
They fought off the Indians
With musket and ball
And reached California
In spite of it all.

Sing toorali—oorali—oorali ay!
Sing toorali—oorali—oorali ay!

I Shall Not Pass This Way Again

ANONYMOUS

Through this toilsome world, alas!

Once and only once I pass;

If a kindness I may show,

If a good deed I may do

To a suffering fellow man,

Let me do it while I can.

No delay, for it is plain

I shall not pass this way again.

PETER PAN

by J. M. Barrie

Once a week Jane's nurse had her evening off; and then it was Wendy's part to put Jane to bed. That was the time for stories. It was Jane's invention to raise the sheet over her mother's head and her own, thus making a tent, and in the awful darkness to whisper:

"What do we see now?"

"I don't think I see anything to-night," says Wendy, with a feeling that if Nana were here she would object to further conversation.

"Yes, you do," says Jane, "you see when you were a little girl."

"That is a long time ago, sweetheart," says Wendy. "Ah me, how time flies!"

"Does it fly," asks the artful child, "the way you flew when you were a little girl?"

"The way I flew! Do you know, Jane, I sometimes wonder whether I ever did really fly."

"Yes, you did."

"The dear old days when I could fly!"

"Why can't you fly now, mother?"

"Because I am grown up, dearest. When people grow up they forget the way."

"Why do they forget the way?"

"Because they are no longer gay and innocent and heartless. It is only the gay and innocent and heartless who can fly."

"What is gay and innocent and heartless? I do with I was gay and innocent and heartless."

Or perhaps Wendy admits that she does see something.

"I do believe," she says, "that it is this nursery."

"I do believe it is," says Jane. "Go on."

They are now embarked on the great adventure of the night when Peter flew in looking for his shadow.

"The foolish fellow," says Wendy, "tried to stick it on with soap, and when he could not he cried, and that woke me, and I sewed it on for him."

"You have missed a bit," interrupts Jane, who now knows the story better than her mother. "When you saw him sitting on the floor crying, what did you say?"

"I sat up in bed and I said, 'Boy, why are you crying?'"

"Yes, that was it," says Jane, with a big breath.

"And then he flew us all away to the Neverland and the fairies and the pirates and the redskins and the mermaids' lagoon, and the home under the ground, and the little house."

"Yes! Which did you like best of all?"

"I think I liked the home under the ground best of all."

"Yes, so do I. What was the last thing Peter ever said to you."

"The last thing he ever said to me was, 'Just always be waiting for me, and then some night you will hear me crowing.'"

"Yes."

"But, alas, he forgot all about me." Wendy said it with a smile. She was as grown up as that.

"What did his crow sound like?" Jane asked one evening.

"It was like this," Wendy said, trying to imitate Peter's crow.

"No, it wasn't," Jane said gravely, "it was like this"; and she did it ever so much better than her mother.

Wendy was a little startled. "My darling, how can you know?"

"I often hear it when I am sleeping," Jane said.

"Ah yes, many girls hear it when they are sleeping, but I was the only one who heard it awake."

"Lucky you," said Jane.

And then one night came the tragedy. It was the spring of the year, and the story had been told for the night, and

Jane was now asleep in her bed. Wendy was sitting on the floor, very close to the fire, so as to see to darn, for there was no other light in the nursery; and while she sat darning she heard a crow. Then the window blew open as of old, and Peter dropped on the floor.

He was exactly the same as ever, and Wendy saw at once that he still had all his first teeth.

He was a little boy, and she was grown up. She huddled by the fire not daring to move, helpless and guilty, a big woman.

"Hullo, Wendy," he said, not noticing any difference, for he was thinking chiefly of himself; and in the dim light her white dress might have been the nightgown in which he had seen her first. "Hullo, Peter," she replied faintly, squeezing herself as small as possible. Something inside her was crying "Woman, woman, let go of me."

"Hullo, where is John?" he asked, suddenly missing the third bed.

"John is not here now," she gasped.

"Is Michael asleep?" he asked, with a careless glance at Jane.

"Yes," she answered; and now she felt that she was untrue to Jane as well as to Peter.

"That is not Michael," she said quickly, lest a judgment should fall on her.

112

Peter looked. "Hullo, is it a new one?"

"Yes."

"Boy or girl?"

"Girl."

Now surely he would understand; but not a bit of it.

"Peter," she said, faltering, "are you expecting me to fly away with you?"

"Of course; that is why I have come." He added a little sternly, "Have you forgotten that this is spring-cleaning time?"

She knew it was useless to say that he had let many spring-cleaning times pass.

"I can't come," she said apologetically, "I have forgotten how to fly."

"I'll soon teach you again."

"O Peter, don't waste the fairy dust on me."

She had risen; and now at last a fear assailed him. "What is it?" he cried, shrinking.

"I will turn up the light," she said, "and then you can see for yourself."

For almost the only time in his life that I know if, Peter was afraid. "Don't turn up the light," he cried.

She let her hands play in the hair of the tragic boy. She was not a little girl heart-broken about him; she was a grown woman smiling at it all, but they were wet smiles.

Then she turned up the light, and Peter saw. He gave a cry of pain; and when the tall beautiful creature stopped to lift him in her arms he drew back sharply.

"What is it?" he cried again.

She had to tell him.

"I am old, Peter. I am ever so much more than twenty. I grew up long ago."

"You promised not to!"

"I couldn't help it. I am a married woman, Peter."

"No, you're not."

"Yes, and the little girl in the bed is my baby."

"No, she's not."

But he supposed she was; and he took a step towards the sleeping child with his dagger upraised. Of course he did not strike. He sat down on the floor instead and sobbed; and Wendy did not know how to comfort him, though she could have done it so easily once. She was only a woman now, and she ran out of the room to try to think.

Peter continued to cry, and soon his sobs woke Jane. She sat up in bed, and was interested at once.

"Boy," she said, "why are you crying?"

Peter rose and bowed to her, and she bowed to him from the bed.

"Hullo," he said.

"Hullo," said Jane.

"My name is Peter Pan," he told her.

"Yes, I know."

"I came back for my mother," he explained, "to take her to the Neverland."

"Yes, I know," Jane said, "I been waiting for you."

When Wendy returned diffidently she found Peter sitting on the bed-post crowing gloriously, while Jane in her nighty was flying round the room in solemn ecstasy.

"She is my mother," Peter explained; and Jane descended and stood by his side, with the look on her face that he liked to see on ladies when they gazed at him.

"He does so need a mother," Jane said.

"Yes, I know," Wendy admitted rather forlornly; "no one knows it so well as I."

"Good-bye," said Peter to Wendy; and he rose in the air, and the shameless Jane rose with him; it was already her easiest way of moving about.

Wendy rushed to the window.

"No, no," she cried.

"It is just for spring-cleaning time," Jane said; "he wants me always to do his spring cleaning."

"If only I could go with you," Wendy sighed.

"You see you can't fly," said Jane.

Of course in the end Wendy let them fly away together. Our last glimpse of her shows her at the window, watching them receding into the sky until they were as small as stars.

ACTIVITIES

Tiny Boats

*A*maze your grandkids with these funny little boats that can be made from almost anything! An empty walnut shell or a broken eggshell can easily become a seafaring vessel. Even the smallest children can make an aluminum-foil boat, and a peanut canoe looks so realistic you won't believe how quick it is to make. Complete your fleet of homemade boats with some matchstick people, and send them sailing the next time there's a rainy day.

WALNUT OR EGGSHELL BOAT

*M*ake a sail by drawing a design or picture on a small piece of paper using crayons or markers. Make two small slits at the top and bottom, and then weave a toothpick through the slits to create a mast. Use craft glue or a small piece of craft gum to attach the toothpick mast to the inside at one end of half a walnut shell for a tiny one-man sea cruiser. You could also use one half of a clean eggshell.

ALUMINUM-FOIL BOAT

*S*tart with a piece of foil approximately 6 inches square. Fold the square in half and slightly scrunch and pinch the two ends closed.

Reopen the boat gently. Stand the boat on a flat surface and use your fingers to flatten the bottom down a little so it will float.

PEANUT CANOE

Cut the top off of a large peanut length-wise, making sure to leave the ends on. Remove the peanut to hollow out the inside. Add a brave little matchstick sailor, and your peanut canoe is ready for action!

MATCHSTICK PEOPLE

Remove a match from a matchbook. Using a pair of scissors, cut a slit in the bottom to about halfway up and slightly separate the two pieces. Be careful not to break them. These will be the legs. Carefully make two slits on either side of the matchstick from the middle up to a lit-tle bit before the match-stick head. These will be the arms. Gently fold the legs to make your match-stick person sit in a boat.

Big Little Boy

BY EVE MERRIAM

"Me oh my," said the tiny, shiny ant,
"I can crawl all the way up a sand hill,
A hill so high it's as big as a thimble.
Can any creature in the world be bigger than I?"

"Skat," said the green caterpillar,
"I can inch myself all the way across a twig.
Now a twig is really big!
Hooray for great, glorious, mammoth,
   and modest me."

"Gog and magog," said the speckled frog,
"And bilge water. Little ant, crawly caterpillar,
You can only creep.
I can leap!
All the way up to a tremendous lily pad in the pond.
How superiffic can any creature be?
I'll tell you—
He can be me!"

"Oh," laughed the little boy,
"Gangway, skedaddle, vamoose.
Look at me, tiny ant. My finger is bigger than a thimble.
Look, inchy caterpillar. My foot is bigger than a twig.
Look, speckled frog. My hand can cover a lily pad all over.
Why, I'm so big I can run in circles, I can run in squares,

I can reach to tables, I can fill up chairs!
And I'm still growing!
When I grow all the way up, my head will bump the sky.
        I'll have clouds for a bed, and a moon pillow,
        And stars instead of freckles on my nose."

            (Is that how big a little boy grows?)

Legendary Tall Tales: The Mission of Johnny Appleseed

there are plenty of stories about tough cowboys, cunning pioneers, and steely lawmen in America. But one of the most famous legends is about a man who wasn't strong or violent or rough. In fact, this man became known far and wide because he was the complete opposite. He was kind and peaceful, and he only wanted to live in harmony with nature and help his fellow men. His name was Johnny Appleseed, and it's because of him that thousands of apple trees grew and prospered in the middle of America.

Many stories are told about Johnny Appleseed. He roamed by himself from New York all the way to Michigan, Ohio, and Illinois. He never bothered to build a house or buy things, and he lived a very peaceful life, traveling through the land.

The American wilderness was a very dangerous place in the late 18th century, before many towns were built, but Johnny didn't carry a knife or a gun, and Native-American tribes didn't attack him. They respected him and let him pass on his way since he never caused trouble and respected the land. Wild animals never frightened him, and once during a fierce blizzard he crawled into an abandoned tree trunk only to encounter a mother bear and her two cubs hibernating inside! Instead of running for the hills, Johnny simply curled up next to them and had a good night's sleep, completely at ease with the enormous creatures beside him.

He did small odd jobs for settlers he met, and only requested some food or old clothing as payment. This sometimes made him look pretty funny, since the clothes often didn't fit, and he usually didn't own shoes and wore a steel pot for a hat! He didn't see the need for fancy clothes or transportation, and instead spent his days traveling on foot or by canoe, living as one with nature and the creatures of the land.

Johnny Appleseed's love and respect for nature included all animals, no matter how fierce or dangerous they were. One day, he came upon a wolf caught in a hunter's trap. The wolf snarled and lunged at Johnny when he approached, but it was obvious the animal was in a lot of pain and pretty exhausted.

"There, there," Johnny said in a low, comforting voice. Bit by bit he made his way toward the wounded animal, and miraculously, the wolf grew calm. Carefully, Johnny pried open the trap and studied the wolf's leg. He was pretty badly hurt, so Johnny gathered medicinal herbs and tore a long bandage from his tattered shirt. He took care of the wolf until the wound healed.

In fact, Johnny took such good care of him that the wolf began following him around like a faithful puppy dog. Johnny finally had to send him back to his den though, as the sight of a ferocious wolf calmly walking by his side had a tendency to scare the willies out of people!

Because Johnny loved his animal friends so much, it often made him sad when he saw people hunting them. He himself only ate vegetables, berries, and grains, but he understood that people needed to have food. Otherwise they would starve. The Midwest was a tough place, and sometimes it was very difficult to plant crops or maintain a farm. People were often hungry and had to rely on what they caught to survive.

"If only there was a way to bring food to the people without having them hunt animals every day or go hungry," Johnny thought as he rested beneath a glorious apple tree, full of beautiful white blossoms. Suddenly he jumped up. "Why, the answer's right in front of my face! I'll collect apple seeds and plant them across this whole great nation. When the apples ripen, everyone will have something to eat. No one will have to go hungry again!" And he began collecting the seeds immediately.

Johnny traveled across several states, planting apple seeds and giving away small trees to settlers as he went. Instead of simply providing people with food once, he gave them the gift of apples, which would grow again and again. Settlers were always eager to see Johnny Appleseed, as they knew that soon enough their kitchens would be full of delicious, juicy apples.

Because of his peaceful ways and kindness, Johnny Appleseed left a permanent mark on America. Even today you can visit the Midwest and view the beautiful apple trees Johnny planted to help make the world a more gentle and loving place. ⟨

ACTIVITIES

Best Tree Swing Ever

On a hot August day, a tire swinging from a strong branch of a big shade tree can be a grandchild's best friend. It only takes a few inexpensive materials to build a sturdy swing that can last for years. Solicit older grandchildren to help you build the perfect swing, while younger ones delight in the creation of a new plaything.

The ideal tree for your swing should have a sturdy branch sprouting directly from the trunk about fifteen or so feet above the ground. Think about location, too. Hilltops make for great views and can be perfect spots for daydreaming. If there's a good swimming hole nearby, look for a strong branch over the water where it's safe to jump in.

The success of any good tree swing comes with a little foresight about wear and tear. By reinforcing the tree limb where you'll be attaching the rope, you can protect the limb from the friction created by the swinging rope and ensure a long life for the swing. And a piece of wood attached to the tire swing where the rope will tie around it will allow the tire to bear the weight of a swinger without collapsing.

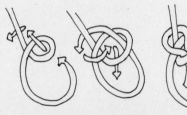

HOW TO TIE A BOWLINE KNOT

Two large rubber tires, strong rope, 2 pieces wood (one about 2" x 2" x 3" and the other about 2" x 4" x 8"), 10-penny nails, a sharp knife

1. On 1 tire, nail the smaller board to the underside of what will be the top of the swing.
2. Nail the larger board opposite the smaller board to create a seat or footstep along the inner bottom of the tire.
4. Cut a small hole out of the very bottom of the tire to allow water to drain out after a rainstorm.
5. Out of the other tire, cut a section of |rubber about ten inches long that will wrap over the top of the tree limb as padding underneath the rope supporting the swing.
6. Tie the rope over the protective rubber with a bowline knot. Nail rope and rubber to secure. Attach the other end of the rope to the tire swing over the smaller piece of wood with another bowline knot. Allow the bottom of the swing to hang about two feet off the ground. Your tire is now ready to swing!

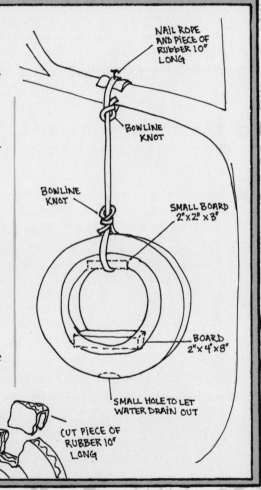

NAIL ROPE AND PIECE OF RUBBER 10" LONG

BOWLINE KNOT

BOWLINE KNOT

SMALL BOARD 2" x 2" x 3"

BOARD 2" x 4" x 8"

SMALL HOLE TO LET WATER DRAIN OUT

CUT PIECE OF RUBBER 10" LONG

He that is good at making excuses
is seldom good at anything else.

—BENJAMIN FRANKLIN

Happiness comes when your work
and your words are of benefit to
yourself and to others.

—BUDDHA

It takes less time to do a thing right
than to explain why you did it wrong.

—HENRY WADSWORTH LONGFELLOW

Laziness may appear attractive,
but work gives satisfaction.

—ANNE FRANK

If you want a job done right, do it yourself.

Don't bite off more than you can chew.

Never leave that till tomorrow which
you can do today.

—Benjamin Franklin

When you are asked if you can
do a job, tell 'em, "Certainly
I can." Then get busy and
find out how to do it.

—Teddy Roosevelt

Where there's a
will there's a way.

—George Herbert

127

Did you ever?

Did you ever see a match box,
or a garden fence?

EZ Soups & Salads

No matter how many grandchildren you have, it pays to master the art of making quick, great-tasting meals using simple, accessible ingredients. Keep the refrigerator stocked with bags of prewashed salad blends as well as lunch meats, cheese, and fruit. Then, when the grandkids pop by for a visit, it's always a cinch to toss together an easy lunch or dinner for everyone.

Split Pea & Sausage Soup

1 (16-ounce) package dried split peas
4 ounces smoked sausage links,
    sliced and quartered
7 cups water
1 onion, chopped
2 carrots, chopped
1 teaspoon salt
1 teaspoon Italian seasoning
$1/2$ teaspoon pepper
Croutons
Parmesan cheese

1. Rinse peas with cold water in colander.
2. Place all ingredients (except croutons and cheese) in 5-quart Dutch oven. Bring to a boil over high heat.
3. Reduce heat and simmer uncovered for about an hour or until peas are tender, stirring occasionally.
4. Remove sausage with slotted spoon and set aside.
5. In 3-cup batches, puree soup with blender or food processor.
6. Return soup and sausage to Dutch oven and reheat over medium flame.
7. Ladle soup into bowls and top with croutons and Parmesan cheese. Serve immediately.

Makes 6 servings

TOO MANY

COOKS

SPOIL

THE

BROTH

Farmhouse Soup

2 pounds green beans, cut in thirds
2 large potatoes, scrubbed and diced
Water
1 cup bacon, diced
1 onion, chopped
Salt and pepper to taste

1. Place beans and potatoes in soup pot and add water until vegetables are just covered. Cook over high heat until simmering, then lower to medium heat.

2. While soup is heating, sauté bacon and onions in large skillet, about 5 minutes or until onions are soft.
3. Add bacon and onion mixture to soup pot and continue cooking soup until potatoes are tender. (Add more water if necessary for desired consistency.)
4. Add salt and pepper to taste. Serve immediately.

Makes 4 servings

Quick-Fix Salad Dressing

3 tablespoons olive oil
1 tablespoon vinegar
1 teaspoon mustard
2 teaspoons mayonnaise
1 teaspoon honey
Salt and pepper to taste

Whisk all ingredients together until blended.

Makes 4 servings

Simple Caesar–y Salad

*1 package Caesar salad mix
with dressing
2 potatoes, peeled and sliced coarsely
2 hard-boiled eggs, quartered,
Anchovies (optional)*

1. Place the potato slices in a soup pot with water to cover. Boil until tender but not mushy. Allow to cool.
2. In a large bowl, toss the Caesar salad with the potatoes and the dressing.
3. Garnish with egg quarters and, for adventurous grandchildren, anchovies.

Makes 4 servings

Peachy Luncheon Salad

*1 bag prewashed romaine lettuce
8 slices turkey or ham, cut in thin strips
$1/2$ cup shredded cheese
2 peaches, sliced
Your favorite salad dressing
(or Quick-Fix Salad Dressing)*

1. Divide the romaine lettuce among 4 bowls.
2. Top each with even amounts of meat, cheese, and peach slices.
3. Drizzle with salad dressing and serve.

Makes 4 servings

Leisure

BY WILLIAM HENRY DAVIES

What is life if, full of care,
We have no time to stand and stare.

No time to stand beneath the boughs
And stare as long as sheep or cows.

No time to see, when woods we pass,
Where squirrels hide their nuts in grass.

No time to see, in broad daylight,
Streams full of stars, like stars at night.

No time to turn at Beauty's glance,
And watch her feet, how they can dance.

No time to wait till her mouth can
Enrich that smile her eyes began.

A poor life this if, full of care,
We have no time to stand and stare.

The Six Sillies

O nce upon a time, there was a young woman who was so foolish that she had never had a boyfriend, and her family worried that she would never get married. They were all very relieved when she finally met a young man and brought him to dinner. Everything was going very well until her mother asked the young woman to go to the kitchen and bring out some more ice for their drinks.

When the young woman never came back, her mother excused herself and went into the kitchen to see what was keeping her daughter. She found the young woman sitting on the floor with her head in her hands, while a large puddle of water grew on the floor. She had forgotten to shut the freezer door and now all the ice was melting.

"What are you doing?" the mother demanded.

"I was thinking of what I will name my first child after I am married to that young man," she said. And then she sighed. "I can't decide on a single name!"

Now, a sensible mother would have told her daughter to get up and stop being so ridiculous. But instead, the young woman's mother sat down next to her. "I will think about it with you, my dear," she said.

After the mother and daughter had not come out of the kitchen for some time, the young woman's father excused himself and went in to see what was wrong. He found both of them sitting on the floor, next to a big puddle of water from the melting ice.

"What on earth is going on in here?" he asked. "You're letting everything in the freezer thaw!"

The Six Sillies

"We were thinking about what our daughter will name her first child once she marries that young man outside. We can't decide on a single name!" the mother replied.

And instead of calling his wife and daughter silly little geese, the old man sat down next to them. "Well, three heads are better than two. I'll help you think of a solution."

After a bit of time had passed, the young man noticed water seeping under the door to the kitchen. He went in to investigate, and found the whole family sitting on the floor, surrounded by water.

"What is going on? Have you all gone crazy?" he asked.

The old man grumbled. "Be still. Can't you see that we're all thinking hard about what you shall name your first child when you marry my daughter? We can't decide on a single name!"

When the young man heard that, he shook his head. "Well,

good-bye! I'm going away now.
When I find three people sillier
than you are, maybe I will come
back and marry your daughter!"

He left the house and began
walking toward his home. In order
to reach it, he had to walk
through a small forest. Beneath
an apple tree, he came across a
woman trying to pick up a bunch
of apples on the ground with a
pitchfork and toss them into
a cart.

"What are you doing?" the
young man asked.

"I want to load my cart with
apples," the woman answered,
"but for some reason, I don't seem
to be getting anywhere."

The young man told her, "Why
don't you gather the apples in a
basket first, and then use *that* to
dump them into your cart?"

After hearing the woman's
thanks for his advice, the young
man thought, "Well, here is certainly one person sillier than

The Six Sillies

those three I left at the house."

The young man continued to walk through the woods until he saw another peculiar sight. A boy wanted to give his pet pig some acorns to eat, and was trying with all of his might to make the pig climb up an oak tree.

"My goodness," said the young man, "What are you doing?"

"I want my pig to eat some acorns, but I can't seem to get him to climb up this tree," the boy told him.

"Well, why don't you climb up the tree and then shake the acorns down for your pig?"

"Oh, I never thought of that," said the boy.

The young man shook his head and walked on. "Well, there's another person who is more foolish than the first three," he thought.

He had almost made it to his house when he saw the strangest sight of all. Tied between two trees was a pair of pants, and as he watched, a man was jumping up with all of his might and trying to get his legs into both pant legs as he came down. This time, he didn't need to ask what the man thought he was doing.

"You know, you'd have much better luck if you simply held the pants in your hands and then put them on, one leg at a time!" he advised him.

"Of course!" shouted the man. "You are much smarter than I am! I would have never thought of that!"

Having found the final person who was more foolish than either the young woman or her parents, the young man turned around and went back to the young lady's house, where he immediately asked her to marry him.

And in time, they had a great many children and decided on names for every single one of them. ✳

A Fairy Tale Verse

Everyone was fast asleep,
Princess, courtiers, cats and sheep,
And there grew a thorny wall
Through which none could come at all.
Thus a hundred years rolled past
Till a royal prince at last
Cut his way through thorns, and they
Turned to roses right away.

Sleeping Beauty

Then he kissed the princess's eyes
And she woke in sweet surprise.
Soon the palace was astir,
Ready to rejoice with her.

When you see me sitting quietly,
Like a sack left on the shelf,
Don't think I need your chattering,
I'm listening to myself.
Hold! Stop! Don't pity me!
Hold! Stop your sympathy!
Understanding if you got it,
Otherwise I'll do without it!

When my bones are stiff and aching
And my feet won't climb the stairs,
I will only ask one favor:
Don't bring me no rocking chair.

When you see me walking, stumbling,
Don't study and get it wrong.
'Cause tired don't mean lazy
And every goodbye ain't gone.
I'm the same person I was back then,
A little less hair, a little less chin,
A lot less lungs and much less wind,
But ain't I lucky I can still breathe in.

On Ageing

BY MAYA ANGELOU

THE BLACK STALLION
by Walter Farley

They approached the barn. Alec saw Henry Dailey leaning against the door watching them. He rode up to him and dismounted, catching hold of the stallion's halter. "Morning, Henry," he said. He felt the Black's coat. "Not even wet. . . . What a horse, Henry! We've been going around that field like the wind! Did you see us?"

Henry didn't move from the door but Alec saw his small gray eyes going over the Black inch by inch. "Sure, I saw you," he said. "Son, I've seen a lot of horses in my day and rode my share of 'em, but I never saw one give any better exhibition than that!"

Alec beamed with pride. "He is swell, Henry, isn't he? I still can't believe he's mine!" The stallion's long neck reached down to the ground and he buried his nose in the green grass.

"Let him loose, Alec. See how he likes it," said Henry.

"Do you think it's safe?"

"He's all right now. You gave him a good run. Besides he has to get used to being left alone, anyway."

"Guess you're right, Henry." Alec unsnapped the lead rope from the halter.

The stallion raised his head and his nostrils quivered. Suddenly he wheeled and trotted swiftly down the field.

Alec and Henry watched him. "It's the first freedom he's had in a long time," said Alec.

"And he's sure enjoying it." Henry looked after the Black admiringly.

The stallion stopped and turned his great head toward them. He whistled softly.

"Boy, I'd love to see him on a track!" Henry said thoughtfully.

"You mean race, Henry?" Alec asked.

"Yep."

Alec turned to the Black, who was now loping down the field again in an easy, graceful canter, his head turning from side to side. "It'd take a long time before he'd be safe on any track though, Henry."

"Well, we have plenty of time, haven't we, Alec?"

"We?" Alec stared at the small husky man beside him. "You mean, Henry, that you and I could do it?"

Henry hadn't moved—his eyes still followed the

Black around the field. "Sure, we can," he said quietly, and then his voice lowered so that Alec could hardly hear him. "Never liked this business of retiring, anyway," he said. "Not too old—still have plenty of good years left in me! This life's all right for the Missus—she's got enough to do to keep her busy, but I need action. And here I have it shoved right into my lap!" His voice grew louder. "Alec," he continued, "I know we can make a champion out of the Black." His face was wrinkled with excitement, his eyelids narrowed until they were only slits in his lined face.

"You really mean it, Henry? But how—"

The old man interrupted him and he moved for the first time. "Sure, I'm confident, Alec, and I know my horses." He took the boy by the arm. "Come with me and I'll show you something."

Henry led him to the far end of the barn. He knelt down beside an old trunk. He took a key from his pocket, inserted it into the lock and opened it. The trunk was crammed to the top with trophies and silver cups. Henry dug down and pulled out a large scrapbook. "The Missus always kept this for me, even before we were married."

He turned the faded yellowish pages that were filled with newspaper clippings. Headline after headline caught Alec's eye as he knelt beside Henry: DAILEY RIDES CHANG TO VICTORY IN SCOTT MEMORIAL—DAILEY BRINGS WARRIOR HOME FIRST IN $50,000 FUTURITY—TURFDOM ACCLAIMS DAILEY AS GREATEST RIDER OF

THE BLACK STALLION

ALL TIME—Henry stopped turning the pages, his eyes gazing steadily at a photograph in front of him. "This, son," he said, "is where I got the greatest thrill of my life—riding Chang home first in the Kentucky Derby. Wouldn't think that little guy there was me, would you?"

Alec looked closer. He saw a small boy, with a wide grin on his face, astride a large, powerful-looking red horse. Around the horse's neck hung the winner's horseshoe of roses. Alec noticed the large, strong hands holding the reins and the stocky, broad shoulders. "Yes," he said, "I can tell that's you."

Henry smiled and reached down into the trunk again. He took out what looked to Alec like old dried-out leaves. Then he saw that they were in the shape of a horseshoe. He looked again at the photograph.

"Yes," Henry said, "it's the same one they placed around Chang's neck that day. Not much left of 'em, but they still hold plenty of memories!"

Henry put the dried flowers back into the trunk. "When I finally got too old and too heavy to ride horses any more, I trained them instead," he continued. "I married the Missus and we were both pretty happy. We had two children—both girls; now they're married. Somehow, I've always missed not having a boy—someone like you, son, who loved horses, and who would sort of follow in my footsteps, because there isn't anything so exciting in the world as lining up there at the post with a four-legged piece of dynamite underneath you!

"Well, to go on, I was pretty successful as a trainer, made good money. And then came the day when the Missus thought it was time for us to retire and get away from the track. Can't say as I blame her, it's the only life she ever knew after she married me, and I guess it wasn't in her blood like it was in mine. We did a lot of movin' around for a good many years, then we bought this place, and here we are. It's been two years since I saw my last race— two years. I don't think I can stand it much longer."

Henry paused again. "You see, Alec," he said, "I'm telling you this to show you that if there is only one thing that I do know anything about it's whether a horse is any good or not—and let me tell you we can make the Black the greatest racer that ever set a hoof on any track!"

Henry closed the book with a sharp crack and placed it back inside the trunk. He rose to his feet and put his hand on the boy's shoulder. "What do you say, son—are you game?"

Alec looked at the old man and then toward the open door where he could see the Black in the distance. "It would be great, Henry!" he said. "And I know he would give any horse in the world a real race—if we can just keep him from fighting."

"It'll be a tough job, Alec, but it's going to be worth it to see him come pounding down the homestretch!" 🏃

The Camptown ladies sing their song,
Doodah, doodah!
The Camptown racetrack's five miles long,
Oh, doodah day!

I come down here with my hat caved in,
Doodah, doodah!
I go back home with a pocket full of tin.
Oh, doodah day!

Chorus
Goin' to run all night, Goin' to run all day.
I'll bet my money on a bobtail nag;
Somebody bet on the bay.

Camptown Races

The longtail filly and the big black horse,
Doodah, doodah!
They fly the track and they both cut across,
Oh, dooday day!

The blind horse stickin' in a big mud hole,
Doodah, doodah!
Can't touch bottom with a ten foot pole
Oh, doodah day!

Chorus

Two of Them

ANONYMOUS

Grandfather's come to see baby to-day,
Dear little, queer little baby Ned;
With his toothless mouth, his double chin,
And never a hair on his shiny head,
He looks in the pretty eyes of blue,
Where the baby's soul is peeping through,
And cries, with many a loving kiss,
'Hallo! what little old man is this?'

Baby stares in grandfather's face,
Merry old, cherry old 'Grandfather Ned,'
With his toothless mouth, his double chin,

And never a hair on his dear old head;
He scans him solemnly up and down,
From his double chin to his smooth, balk crown,
And says to himself as babies do,
'Hallo! can this be a baby, too?'

LEGENDARY TALL TALES: THE MIGHTY BIG STORY OF PAUL BUNYAN

Once upon a time, there lived a very famous lumberjack named Paul Bunyan. Now, when Paul was born, he looked like any other baby. But he started growing at an amazing pace, and within a week, he had to wear his father's clothes. By the time he was a child, he had to use wagon wheels for buttons!

Paul Bunyan grew bigger and bigger, until finally his family began to worry that they wouldn't be able to afford to feed and clothe him anymore.

"Now son," his father said, "you know we love you, but, well, it looks like you're getting a little too large for this family." He had to use a megaphone so Paul could hear his words that high up in the air. "Maybe it's time you stepped out and had a look at this great big country."

"Oh Paul." His mother wept and stepped into his hand so he could bring her up to his face for a kiss. Paul hated leaving his little family, but he knew they were right. Ever since he was little, something in his heart wouldn't let him feel satisfied. Maybe if he went out into the wide world, he might find out what it was he wanted someday.

Saying goodbye was hard, but he was careful not to cry—otherwise he would have flooded the entire area! Paul promised to keep in touch, and then he packed up his few belongings and strode off into the wilderness. The ground shook with each giant step he took.

After walking for a while, Paul started to feel very sad and lonely. He lay down on the ground and looked up into the deep blue sky. "This wouldn't be so bad," he thought, "if I only had a friend to travel with me." He drifted off to sleep, but suddenly woke up when he felt something rough and wet on his face. He opened his eyes and was amazed to find a giant ox licking him. Not only was the ox as big as Paul, but he was bright blue as well, as if he had just stepped down from out of the sky! Paul had no idea how he had come there, but he was grateful for a

friend. He named the ox Babe, and from that day forth, the two were inseparable.

The pair traveled all over the country, shaping it wherever they went. Their giant footprints became the 10,000 lakes of Minnesota when they filled with rainwater. And he dug out the Grand Canyon just so he and Babe could take a bath!

Weather was odd back then, and one

year the country had two winters. Because his head was as high as a mountaintop, Paul found he couldn't make a sound since his words froze stiff as soon as they came out of his mouth. It wasn't until the spring that his words thawed, and then the air rang with his chatter for a whole week! Paul and Babe thought this was so funny that they fell on the ground and rolled from side to side, and that's how the Black Hills of South Dakota were formed.

Yes, Paul was certainly having a grand time with Babe, but he still was not content and he couldn't exactly say why.

One day, as he was strolling through Oregon picking up huge boulders as if they were pebbles and skipping them across lakes, he walked right into the middle of a loggers' camp. All of the men were startled to see giant Paul, but they were so busy worrying that they barely shouted out a greeting.

"Hey, you," Paul called to a man by his feet. "Why's everyone so glum?"

The man said, "We're all worried about our jobs. We're supposed to cut down two hundred trees by tomorrow, but everyone's sick with the whooping cough and can't work." He wrung his hands. "We're all going to get fired, and then what will we tell our families?'

"Two hundred trees, huh?" Paul said, half to himself. "Why, I bet I could cut down those trees for you in about two hours."

Then, taking two of the giant blades from a woodcutting machine, he fashioned two axes and set off for the forest. "Come on, Babe!" he called, "we've got work to do!"

And work they did. All you could hear for miles around was the *Woosh!* of Paul's axes whistling through the air and the *Crash!* as trees fell. Although he cut down an incredible amount, he was careful to leave the young trees to grow, and he didn't harm any of the other parts of the forest. Babe caught all of the logs Paul tossed to him on his broad back and tugged them into a pile.

Before Paul had even broken a sweat, there were the two hundred logs, neatly stacked and ready to go. All of the men from the logging camp cheered!

"Thanks Paul!" they all called up.

Paul smiled to himself at the work he had done. "You know, Babe, I think this might just be the job for me." And so he stayed on at the logging camp, helping to clear the forest and produce wood for the growing country. No one could beat Paul Bunyan in any contest of strength, and he and Babe always had the most logs cut by the end of the day.

Paul made a lot of friends at the logging camp and had a good time traveling with them. In fact, the only one who sometimes grumbled was the cook. In order to make Paul's flapjacks, he had to heat up a skillet a mile long, and then have ten men strap pats of butter to their feet to grease it! Twenty men had to work together to flip each flapjack, and then Paul would come along and eat them all up in about a minute! The cook would fling up his hands and take to his bed for the rest of the day, but everyone else in the camp thought this was hilarious.

And so, Paul Bunyan finally felt satisfied as he worked hard with his blue ox and his friends from the camps. The stories about him grew and grew, much like Paul did when he was a little boy, until finally his were the tallest tales of all! ⋏

From the great Atlantic Ocean
To the wide Pacific shore,
From sunny California
To ice-bound Labrador,
She's mighty tall and handsome,
She's known quite well by all,
She's the 'boes' accommodation
On the Wabash Cannonball

Chorus
Listen to the jingle,
The rumble and the roar,
As she glides along the woodlands,
Through hills and by the shore
Hear the mighty rush of the engine,
Hear those lonesome hoboes squawl,
While traveling through the jungle
On the Wabash Cannonball

She came down from Birmingham
One cold December day,
As she rolled into the station,
You could hear the people say,
There's a girl from Birmingham,
She's long and she is tall,
She come down from Birmingham on
The Wabash Cannonball

Chorus

162

This train, she runs to Memphis,
Mattoon, and Mexico,
She rolls through East St. Louis
And she never does it slow,
As she flies through Colorado,
She gives an awful squawl,
They tell her by her whistle
The Wabash Cannonball

Chorus

Our eastern states are dandy,
So the people always say,
From New York to St. Louis
And Chicago by the way,
From the hills of Minnesota
Where the rippling waters fall,
No changes can be taken
On the Wabash Cannonball

Chorus

Now here's to Boston Blackey,
May his name forever stand,
And always be remembered
By the 'boes throughout the land,
His earthly days are over
And the curtains 'round him fall,
We'll carry him home to victory
On the Wabash Cannonball

The Wabash Cannonball

165

The Field of Corn

An old man had a field, and when he became very ill he sent for his three sons to tell them how to divide it up when he died. "My boys," the old man said, "there's one thing that I want you to do. I have left a rich gift for all of you, but you'll have to search for it in the field." Before they could ask any questions, the old man passed away. The three sons were heartbroken, and didn't even think of the gift their father had left them for many days. But eventually, thoughts of treasure and gold seeped into their minds and they decided to dig up the field to look for the gift. They worked hard and dug up all the soil, but didn't find anything. "That's so weird," one son said. "Why would Dad tell us there was something in this field? We haven't found a single coin or jewel." His brother sighed. "Well, we've already dug the field up. We might as well plant some corn here and make the most of it." So the brothers planted, and the next season, they had a field of beautiful, rich, golden corn, ten times bigger than any crop that had grown when their father planted. Suddenly, each of the sons realized that the gift their father had wanted to give them wasn't riches or jewels, but the joy of seeing their hard work pay off.

Moral: Search until you find, and your hard work will be rewarded.

It Can Be Done

ANONYMOUS

The man who misses all the fun
Is he who says, "It can't be done."
In solemn pride he stands aloof
And greets each venture with reproof.
Had he the power he'd efface
The history of the human race;
We'd have no radio or motor cars,
No streets lit by electric stars;
No telegraph nor telephone,
We'd linger in the age of stone.
The world would sleep if things were run
By men who say, "It can't be done."

Four and Twenty Blackbirds

by Frances Lillian Taylor

Once there was a king who was very fond of good dinners. One day he sent for his chief cook.

"Make ready for a feast," said the king. "Let there be many dishes. And last of all set before me a new kind of food."

The cook went away in great trouble, for she could think of nothing new.

Now, the cook was a great friend to the birds. Every day she filled her pocket with grains of rye to scatter by the wayside.

A little bird heard what the king had said. He told the other birds. Very soon a blackbird came flying to the kitchen window.

"I am king of the blackbirds!" he said. "The good cook has fed me and my people. Now we will help her."

"What shall I do, O king of the blackbirds?" asked the cook.

"Get a pie platter as large as a tub," said the bird. "And make two crusts for a pie." So the dish was brought and the crusts baked.

"Place branches bearing ripe cherries in the pie," said the bird. And it was done.

Then the king of the blackbirds called. Four and twenty blackbirds heard the call. They flew into the pie and hid among the cherry branches.

The feast was made ready. Last of all the great pie was set before the king.

"Here is a new dish, indeed," said the king as he opened the pie.

Then the twenty-four blackbirds began to sing. And their song was all about the good cook and her pocket of rye.

"Send the cook to me," said the king.

The cook came, and, behold, her pocket was full of grains of rye for the birds.

"Change every grain of rye to a silver sixpence," said the king. "And after this let the birds be fed every day."

Then the blackbirds sang a new song. All the people learned it and sang it again and again.

And it was sung into a book and it shall be sung to you.

Sing a song of sixpence,
A pocket full of rye;
Four and twenty blackbirds
Baked in a pie.
When the pie was opened
The birds began to sing;
Was not this a dainty dish
To set before a king?

Kitchen-Sink Pizzas

Announce "Pizza!" and you have a surefire way to get even the pickiest of picky eaters excited about lunch or dinner. You can make pizza out of just about anything in the pantry or refrigerator, including leftovers! Use English muffins, focaccia, frozen crescent rolls, pita bread—you can even make pizza sandwiches. Even when the cupboard is bare, you can usually drum up a little marinara sauce and shredded cheese, and you've got pizza. Try variations on some of these nontraditional recipes, and taste the goodness of your own Kitchen-Sink Pizzas.

Crunchy Crescent Pizzas

1 (8-ounce) can crescent rolls
6 ounces cream cheese
Assorted sliced or chopped raw veggies (broccoli, cucumber, cauliflower, zucchini, squash, peppers, alfalfa sprouts, snap peas, carrots)
Assorted sliced or chopped raw fruit (melon, strawberries, kiwi, banana, apple, grapes, blueberries, mango)

1. Preheat oven to 400°F.
2. Roll out crescent dough pieces evenly into one single sheet on a 10- x 15-inch baking sheet. Press dough with fingertips to eliminate seams between the segments. Prick dough with fork in several places.
3. Bake for 10 minutes or until golden. Cool on wire rack.
4. Spread cream cheese evenly over crust.
5. Let your grandchildren make faces or funny patterns with the fruit and vegetable toppings.
6. Slice into squares, and serve cold.

Makes 6 to 8 servings

Mediterranean Pita Pizzas

4 whole-wheat pitas
*8 tablespoons tapenade (a spread
made with black olives, capers,
and anchovies)*
1 medium-size red onion, sliced
1 large tomato, sliced
8 ounces feta cheese
Dried basil
Dried oregano

1. Preheat oven to 375°F.
2. Cut through each pita to make
   2 rounds. Arrange pita halves
   on nonstick baking sheet.
3. Spread 1 tablespoon tapenade
   on each pita round. Layer each
   round with equal amounts of
   onion, tomato, and cheese.
   Sprinkle tops with dried basil
   and oregano to taste.
4. Bake for 10 minutes.

Makes 4 servings

Spud Pizzas

4 baking potatoes
2 tomatoes, sliced
10 ounces mozzarella cheese, sliced
4 slices Canadian bacon, cut in strips
Italian seasoning to taste
Olive oil for drizzling
Salt and pepper to taste

1. Preheat broiler.
2. Scrub potatoes and prick several
   times with a fork.
3. Cook potatoes in microwave on
   high for 10 to 12 minutes until
   done, rotating halfway through.
4. Cut three slits into each potato
   and stuff each slit with tomato,
   cheese, and bacon.
5. Sprinkle a dash of Italian seasoning into each slit, then drizzle
   olive oil on tops of potatoes. Add
   salt and pepper to taste.
6. Broil spud pizzas for about 5
   minutes, or until cheese is melted.

Makes 4 servings

Leftover-Lovers' Pizza

1 large prepared pizza crust
1 cup leftover spaghetti sauce
(homemade or ready-made)
$1/2$ cup leftover cooked hamburger,
soyburger, or shredded chicken
or turkey
$1/2$ cup salad greens or fresh (or
thawed and dried) spinach
1 cup shredded mozzarella cheese
2 tablespoons olive oil
Cornmeal

1. Preheat oven to 400°F.
2. Spread sauce evenly on top of
   prepared pizza crust.
3. Top with meat, greens, and cheese.
4. Drizzle olive oil on top.
5. Sprinkle a small handful of cornmeal on a pizza stone or baking
   sheet and place pizza on top.
6. Bake for 20 minutes or until crust
   is brown and cheese is melted.

Makes 2 or 3 servings

Surprise!

BY SHEL SILVERSTEIN

My Grandpa went to Myrtle Beach

And sent us back a turtle each.

And then he went to Katmandu

And mailed a real live Cockatoo.

From Rio an iguana came,

A smelly goat arrived from Spain.

Now he's in India, you see—

My Grandpa always thinks of me.

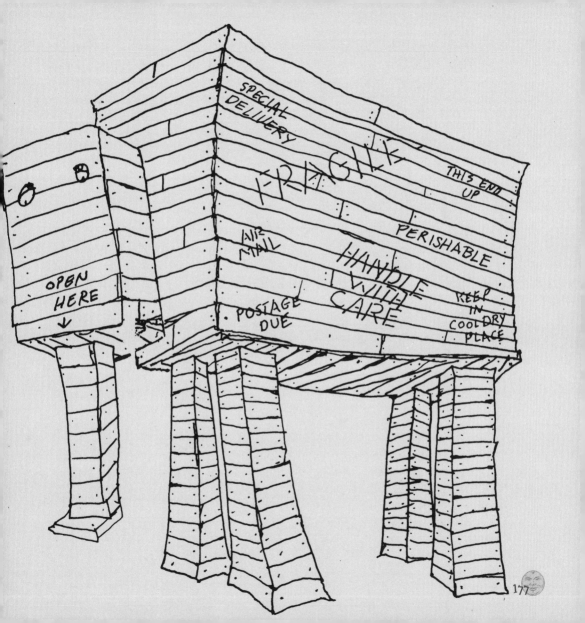

There's a dark and a troubled side of life,
There's a bright and a sunny side, too;
Though you meet with the
   darkness and strife,
The sunny side may also find you.

Chorus
Keep on the sunny side, always on the sunny side,
Keep on the sunny side of life;
It will help us ev'ry day, it will brighten all the way,
If we keep on the sunny side of life

Oh, the storm and its fury broke today,
Crushing hopes that we cherish so dear;
Clouds and storms will in time pass away,
The sun again will shine bright and clear.

Chorus

Let us greet with a song of hope each day,
Though the moment be cloudy or fair;
Let us trust in our Saviour away,
Who keepeth ev'ry one in His care.

Chorus

Keep
On the
Sunny Side

What the Old Man Does Is Always Right

Once upon a time, an old couple lived on a small farm. They didn't have much money or many possessions, but they were comfortable. In fact, the only thing they owned that had much value was a gray-spotted mule. They used the mule for all of the farm jobs, and also to take them to and from town. But as they got older, they realized that they could no longer take care of the mule very well, and so agreed to trade it for something more useful.

"Now, old man, you are always right," said the wife. "Why don't you take the mule to the market and see what you can trade him for?"

The old man agreed, and set off for the market the very next day. It was very hot and dusty, and a few other travelers on the road were also headed to the market. Among these other travelers was a man leading a fat, sturdy sheep with a thick layer of fleece on its back.

"Why, if I traded the mule for that sheep, my wife can make us thick sweaters and blankets for the coming winter!" thought the old man. So, he called over the man with the sheep, and had soon struck a bargain to trade the mule for it.

Since he had already gotten rid of the mule, the old man could have turned back to the farm. But being as how he had set his mind on going on to the market, he continued on his way, this time leading a sheep.

Soon came upon a woman holding a large, fat goose with snowy, white feathers. "Oh, if my wife had that goose, imagine the pillows she could stuff with those feathers!" he thought. And the very thought of sleeping on soft, downy pillows was so appealing that he traded the sheep to the woman with the goose on the spot.

Now, the road to the market was getting very crowded indeed, and the man was amazed to see a brightly colored hen running here and there between the people. "What a beautiful hen!" the old man thought. "Her tail feathers are so bright and she clucks so nicely. Hens are excellent things to have on a farm because they eat up any crumbs and they practically take care of themselves."

At this, he asked the man who owned the hen if he would trade for the goose, and the man of course said yes. The old man was about to turn back when he reached the very gates of the market. He saw a man with a large sack.

"My, it is hot out!" the old man told him. "I've had quite a day so far, and I haven't even been to the market yet!"

"I've had no luck so far, my friend," replied the stranger, "All I have to sell is this sack of rotten apples, but I'm afraid I'll just have to toss them to the pigs!"

"That seems like a terrible waste," the old man mused. "My wife hates to waste things, and I'm sure she would be very distressed about you throwing those apples out. Will you trade the apples for this hen?" Hardly

What the Old Man Does Is Always Right

believing his luck, the man quickly agreed.

After the long trip, the old man felt very hot and thirsty, so he went to the nearest restaurant to get something to eat and drink. Inside, many people were eating and talking about the purchases they had made or the things they had exchanged. The old man had just ordered his food, when two wealthy men sitting at the table next to him began to talk to him.

"You look like you did well today," one man said to him, motioning to the sack. "What's it full of?"

"Rotten apples," said the old man, and he told them the whole story, starting with how he set out that morning to trade the mule.

"So what you're saying is that you've managed to trade a mule for a bag of rotten apple?" One of the men chuckled. "Oh no, when you get home your wife is really going to yell at you!"

"No, she won't," said the old man. "She'll give me a kiss and say, 'My husband is always right.'"

The two rich men were so sure that his wife would yell at him that they said they would give him a bag of gold coins if she did not. After they had finished eating, they all returned to the old man's farm.

"Hello, my husband!" called the old woman. "What have you traded the mule for?"

The old man put down his sack. "I traded our good mule for a wooly sheep."

"Think of all the lovely sweaters and blankets I can knit!" she said.

"But a little farther on, I saw a

goose with snowy white feathers—"

"I love feather pillows!" said the old woman.

"But then after that, I saw the prettiest little hen, and knew you'd love her," the old man replied.

The woman nodded. "Yes, I was just thinking about how wonderful it would be to have scrambled eggs for breakfast!"

The old man finished: "But when I came to the market, I met a man who had a sackful of rotten apples that he was going to throw out. I know how much you hate to waste things, so I traded the hen for the apples, and that's what's in the sack!"

There was silence for a moment, and the two rich men nodded and smiled knowingly. But then the old woman reached up and placed a kiss on the old man's bald head!

She said, "You know, it's funny. After you left, I thought how nice it would be if I baked a cake before you got back. I had the

milk and the eggs, but no flour. So I went to our neighbor to borrow some. But our neighbor is so stingy that she wouldn't give me any of her flour, and told me, 'How can I lend you something when I have so little myself? Why, I barely have an old, shriveled apple in my house!'" Here the old woman laughed, "But now I have a whole sackful of shriveled apples that I can lend to her!"

The two old folks laughed, and the rich men, who were at first astounded, had to join in. "Well, I like all this," said one, "always going down the hill, and yet always merry; it's worth the money to see it." And they gave not one, but three bags of gold coins to the old man who, whatever he did, was not scolded but kissed.

So the old couple had enough money to buy a sheep, and a goose, and a hen, or anything else they wanted, and they lived very happily together. ✹

Things to Think

BY ROBERT BLY

Think in ways you've never thought before
If the phone rings, think of it as carrying a message
Larger than anything you've ever heard,
Vaster than a hundred lines of Yeats.

Think that someone may bring a bear to your door,
Maybe wounded and deranged; or think that a moose
Has risen out of the lake, and he's carrying on his antlers
A child of your own whom you've never seen.

When someone knocks on the door, think that he's about
To give you something large: tell you you're forgiven,
Or that it's not necessary to work all the time, or that it's
Been decided that if you lie down no one will die.

The Goose
with the
Golden Eggs

Once upon a time, an old farmer and his wife discovered they had a goose that laid one beautiful egg made of solid gold each morning. At first they were overjoyed, but then they thought that it was pretty slow work for the goose to lay only one egg a day. They thought all the eggs must be stored inside the goose, so they cut her up to get the eggs. To their dismay, they didn't find any golden eggs, and the goose was just like any other goose. Instead of having one golden egg a day, they now had no eggs at all.

Moral: Those who always want more often end up with nothing at all.

Mother Holle

Once upon a time, there was a woman who had two daughters. One of them was good and hardworking, and the other was selfish and lazy. For some strange reason, the mother loved the bad one best, and made the good daughter do all the work in the house. She had to wash the dishes, sweep the floor, take out the garbage, and do whatever her mother said, and she was never thanked once! Meanwhile the bad daughter was allowed to sleep late and do nothing all day long. The good daughter wasn't even allowed to buy new clothes, so she had to mend any rips she made in her shirts or pants.

Although she loved her mother and sister, the good daughter felt very sad that she was treated so unfairly. One day, she was sitting by the little wishing well in their backyard, trying to sew up a tear in her shirt, when she dropped the spool of thread. Before she realized it, she had reached too far, and tumbled down the well!

She woke up in a beautiful field full of gorgeous flowers and bright sunshine. "Where have I fallen to?" she wondered, and began to walk around. Before she had gone very far, she saw a very strange thing: In the middle of the field was an oven. And coming from the oven was a chorus of voices calling out, "Help us! Help us! If we stay in here much longer, we'll burn!"

The girl immediately opened the oven and pulled out a tray of gingerbread cookies, which then thanked her for her kindness.

"This is definitely a strange place!" she thought. A little farther on, she again heard a voice, this time coming from a grove of trees.

"Oh, please help me! My branches are so heavy with ripe apples, I can hardly hold them up!" one tree declared. Carefully,

Mother Holle

the girl climbed the tree and picked all the ripe apples. Then she placed them in a neat pile, as the tree thanked her.

"What will I find next?" she wondered. And the next thing she saw was a little house, with an old woman sitting on the porch. The woman had thick, bushy eyebrows and such big teeth that the girl became frightened and started to run away.

"Wait a minute!" called the old woman. "You've nothing to be afraid of! I saw what you did for the cookies and the tree. Come back and stay with me, and I will take good care of you!"

Although the old woman's face was still frightening, her voice was so gentle and comforting that the girl could not resist turning back.

"That's a good girl! If you promise to keep my house clean, I will give you everything you ever wanted, and you'll be happy forever and ever! The only thing you must be sure to do is to shake the feather pillows on my bed very well. Nobody likes a lumpy pillow! Make sure all the feathers fly around. When the feathers fly, the people of earth say it is snowing." At this, the girl realized she was talking to Mother Holle, a powerful being.

"I will work as hard as I can," said the girl. And she did.

Every day she made sure the little house was spick-and-span, and that the pillows were always well beaten. She shook them so much that it looked like a snow-storm right in the house! Mother Holle was so impressed that she gave the girl many presents and treated her like her very own daughter.

The girl was happy at first, but for some reason, she began to get homesick. "Mother Holle," she said one day, "I love being with you, but I miss my mother and sister, even if they don't treat me very well. Could I please go back to them?"

Mother Holle nodded. "You've worked very hard here, and I'm sorry to see you go. But I understand how you'd like to go back to your family. I will take you back myself."

She led the girl through the gate at the front of her house, and just as they walked through, something magical happened. Suddenly, a beautiful shower of golden sunshine fell over the girl,

and when she came out, her skin sparkled like gold and her pockets were full of jewels!

"That is your reward for being such a good worker," said Mother Holle.

When the girl returned to her mother and sister, her family was amazed at her beautiful skin and overjoyed at the riches she brought back. A rooster in the yard crowed, "Cock-a-doodle-doo! Your golden daughter's come back to you!"

When her mother heard how the girl had been transformed, she immediately wanted the same thing for her other daughter, the lazy one. The next day, she made her go to the well and drop a spool of thread in. Then she made her leap after it.

Like her sister, the lazy daughter woke up in a field of beautiful flowers. And she walked until she came to the same oven. "Help us! Help us! Or we will burn!" called the cookies, but the lazy daughter just laughed. "Do you think I'm

getting my hands dirty for you? Please!" And she kept walking.

Soon she came to the apple tree. "Oh, please pick these ripe apples. I can barely keep my branches up!" it called.

"Yeah, right," said the lazy daughter. "I could fall down and break a leg." So she ignored the apple tree and came to the little house.

She wasn't afraid of the fearful face of Mother Holle, since she had heard all about her from her sister.

"Do not be afraid," said Mother Holle, "If you work hard and make sure to shake—"

"Okay, okay, okay!" said the impatient girl, "I already know about this. Can I get started working for you?"

The first day, the girl was obedient and tried to do a good job taking care of the house, but by the second day, the dishes weren't done, the floor was a mess, and she had forgotten to shake the pillows of Mother Holle's bed. By the third day, she didn't even bother to get out of her own bed!

"I think it's time for you to go," said Mother Holle.

"Finally!" said the girl, jumping up. As they made their way to the gate, she couldn't wait for the riches she would receive. But instead of being showered with golden sunlight, a storm of black, sticky oil fell on her head! And when she put her hand in her pocket, instead of pulling out jewels, she pulled out toads and snakes!

"That is in return for your service," declared Mother Holle, and shut the gate on her.

The girl struggled to find her way home with the sticky oil in her eyes, and as she came to her house, the rooster crowed, "Cock-a-doodle-doo! Your dirty daughter's come back to you!"

And so in this way, each daughter got exactly what she deserved. ✴

Grandfather Wisdoms

The time is always ripe for doing right.

—MARTIN LUTHER KING, JR.

A clean conscience makes a soft pillow.

No act of kindness, no
matter how small,
is ever wasted.

—AESOP

No one is useless in this world who
lightens the burden of others.

—CHARLES DICKENS

Always do right. This will gratify
some people and astonish the rest.

—MARK TWAIN

Three things in human life are important:
the first is to be kind. The second is to be
kind. The third is to be kind.

—HENRY JAMES

Deal with yourself as an individual
worthy of respect, and make everyone
else deal with you the same way.

—NIKKI GIOVANNI

Let every man be respected as an individual
and no man idolized.

—ALBERT EINSTEIN

Never bend your head. Always hold it high.
Look the world straight in the eye.

—HELEN KELLER

A Fairy Tale Verse

Cinderella sits in tears
Till the fairy dame appears;
Then in satin, after all,
Off she flutters to the ball.
There she has a lovely time
Till the bells at midnight chime;
Hastily she runs to find

Cinderella

For her coach a pumpkin rind;
But her shoe, left on the stair,
No one in the world can wear
Save the kitchen maiden, who
Makes the prince's dream come true.

Dreams

BY ELLA YOUNG

I went sailing
Over the sea,
White gulls and grey gulls
Following me.

Pale sea-palaces
Under my prow,
Trees with gold apples
On every bough!

Golden fishes,
Silver and blue,
Swam before me
Two and two,

Till a wave of Faery,
Curling white,
Whelmed my boat
In rainbow light.

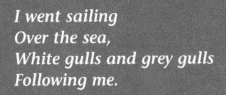

CHARLIE AND THE CHOCOLATE FACTORY

by Roald Dahl

In the evenings, after he had finished his supper of watery cabbage soup, Charlie always went into the room of his four grandparents to listen to their stories, and then afterwards to say good night.

Every one of these old people was over ninety. They were as shriveled as prunes, and as bony as skeletons, and throughout the day, until Charlie made his appearance, they lay huddled in their one bed, two at either end, with nightcaps on to keep their heads warm, dozing the time away with nothing to do. But as soon as they heard the door opening, and heard Charlie's voice saying, "Good evening, Grandpa Joe and Grandma Josephine, and Grandpa George and Grandma Georgina," then all four of them would suddenly sit up, and their old wrinkled faces would light up with smiles of pleasure—and the talking would begin. For they loved this little boy. He was the only bright thing in their lives, and his evening visits were something that they looked forward to all day long. Often, Charlie's mother and father would come in as well, and stand by the door, listening to the stories that the old people told; and thus, for perhaps half an hour every night, this room would become a happy place, and the whole family would forget that it was hungry and poor.

One evening, when Charlie went in to see his grandparents, he said to them, "Is it *really* true that Wonka's Chocolate Factory is the biggest in the world?"

"*True?*" cried all four of them at once. "Of course it's true! Good heavens, didn't you know *that*? It's about *fifty* times as big as any other!"

"And is Mr. Willy Wonka *really* the cleverest chocolate maker in the world?"

"My *dear* boy," said Grandpa Joe, raising himself up a little higher on his pillow, "Mr. Willy Wonka is the most *amazing*, the most *fantastic*, the most *extraordinary* chocolate maker the world has ever seen! I thought *everybody* knew that!"

"I knew he was famous, Grandpa Joe, and I knew he was very clever. . . ."

"*Clever!*" cried the old man. "He's more than that! He's a *magician* with chocolate! he can make *anything*—anything he wants! Isn't that a fact, my dears?"

The other three old people nodded their heads slowly up and down, and said, "*Absolutely* true. *Just* as true as can be."

CHARLIE AND THE CHOCOLATE FACTORY

And Grandpa Joe said, "You mean to say I've never *told* you about Mr. Willy Wonka and his factory?"

"Never," answered little Charlie.

"Good heavens above! I don't know what's the matter with me!"

"Will you tell me now, Grandpa Joe, please?"

"I certainly will. Sit down beside me on the bed, my dear, and listen carefully."

Grandpa Joe was the oldest of the four grandparents. He was ninety-six and a half, and that is just about as old as anybody can be. Like all extremely old people, he was delicate and weak, and throughout the day he spoke very little. But in the evenings, when Charlie, his beloved grandson, was in the room, he seemed in some marvelous way to grow quite young again. All his tiredness fell away from him, and he became as eager and excited as a young boy.

"Oh, what a man he is, this Mr. Willy Wonka!" cried Grandpa Joe. "Did you know, for example, that he has himself invented more than two hundred new kinds of candy bars, each with a different center, each far sweeter and creamier and more delicious than anything the other chocolate factories can make!"

"Perfectly true!" cried Grandma Josephine. "And he sends them to *all* the four corners of the earth! Isn't that so, Grandpa Joe?"

"It is, my dear, it is. And to all the kings and presidents of the world as well. But it isn't only candy bars that he makes. Oh, dear me, no! He has some really *fantastic* inventions up his sleeve, Mr. Willy Wonka has! Did you know that he's invented a way of making chocolate ice cream so that it stays cold for hours and hours without being in the icebox? You can even leave it lying in the sun all morning on a hot day and it won't go runny!"

"But that's *impossible!*" said little Charlie, staring at his grandfather.

"Of course it's impossible!" cried Grandpa Joe. "It's completely *absurd!* But Mr. Willy Wonka has done it!"

"Quite right!" the others agreed, nodding their heads. "Mr. Wonka has done it."

"And then again," Grandpa Joe went on, speaking very slowly now so that Charlie wouldn't miss a word, "Mr. Willy Wonka can make marshmallows that taste of violets, and rich caramels that change color every ten seconds as you suck them, and little feathery sweets that melt away deliciously the moment you put them between your lips. He can make chewing gum that never loses its taste, and candy balloons that you can blow up to enormous sizes before you pop them with a pin and gobble them up. And, by a most secret method, he can make lovely blue birds' eggs with black spots on them, and when you put one of these in your mouth, it gradually gets smaller and smaller until suddenly there is nothing left except a tiny little pink sugary baby bird sitting on the tip of your tongue."

Grandpa Joe paused and ran the point of his tongue slowly over his lips. "It makes my mouth water just *thinking* about it," he said.

"Mine, too," said little Charlie. "But *please* go on."

While they were talking, Mr. and Mrs. Bucket, Charlie's mother and father, had come quietly into the room, and now both were standing just inside the door, listening.

"Tell Charlie about that crazy Indian prince," said Grandma Josephine. "He'd like to hear that."

"You mean Prince Pondicherry?" said Grandpa Joe, and he began chuckling with laughter.

"*Completely* dotty!" said Grandpa George.

"But *very* rich," said Grandma Georgina.

"What did he do?" asked Charlie eagerly.

"Listen," said Grandpa Joe, "and I'll tell you."

"Prince Pondicherry wrote a letter to Mr. Willy Wonka," said Grandpa Joe, "and asked him to come all the way out to India and build him a colossal palace entirely out of chocolate."

204

"Did Mr. Wonka do it, Grandpa?"

"He did, indeed. And what a palace it was! It had one hundred rooms, and *everything* was made of either dark or light chocolate! The bricks were chocolate, and the cement holding them together was chocolate, and the windows were chocolate, and all the walls and ceilings were made of chocolate, so were the carpets and the pictures and the furniture and the beds; and when you turned on the taps in the bathroom, hot chocolate came pouring out.

"When it was all finished, Mr. Wonka said to Prince Pondicherry, 'I warn you, though, it won't last very long, so you'd better start eating it right away.'

"'Nonsense!' shouted the Prince. 'I'm not going to eat my palace! I'm not even going to nibble the staircase or lick the walls! I'm going to *live* in it!'

"But Mr. Wonka was right, of course, because soon after this, there came a very hot day with a boiling sun, and the whole palace began to melt, and then it sank slowly to the ground, and the crazy prince, who was dozing in the living room at the time, woke up to find himself swimming around in a huge brown sticky lake of chocolate."

Little Charlie sat very still on the edge of the bed, staring at his grandfather. Charlie's face was bright, and his eyes were stretched so wide you could see the whites all around. "Is all this *really* true?" he asked. "Or are you pulling my leg?"

"It's true!" cried all four of the old people at once. "Of course it's true! Ask anyone you like!" 🏃

Old-time Quenchers

On a hot summer day, old-fashioned coolers never go out of style. Nothing tastes quite as good as fresh-squeezed lemonade from the fruit of the backyard tree, or ginger ale made with freshly chopped ginger. Share these generational thirst quenchers with your grandchildren and let them have fun "juicing up" at a neighborhood barbecue or roadside lemonade stand (see page 210).

Roadside Lemonade

$1^1/_2$ cups sugar
6 cups water
$1^1/_2$ cups fresh-squeezed lemon juice
(about 8 to 10 lemons)
Ice cubes

1. Mix sugar and 2 cups water in large saucepan and bring to a boil.
2. Reduce heat and simmer, stirring occasionally, until sugar dissolves.
4. Remove from heat and cool.
5. Stir juice into syrup.
6. Stir the above mixture into remaining water in $2^1/_2$-quart container. Refrigerate until cold.
7. Serve in tall glasses over ice cubes.

Makes about 2 quarts

LIMEADE: Substitute limes for lemons.

ORANGEADE: Decrease lemon juice to 1 cup. Substitute 4 cups fresh-squeezed orange juice for the 4 cups of water in step 6.

GRAPEFRUITADE: Decrease lemon juice to $1/_2$ cup. Substitute 4 cups fresh-squeezed grapefruit juice for the water in step 6.

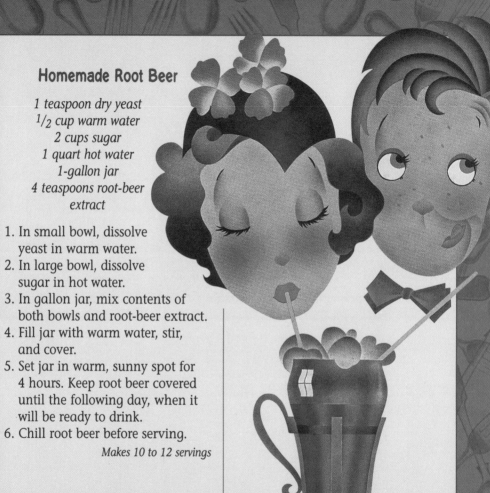

Homemade Root Beer

1 teaspoon dry yeast
$1/2$ cup warm water
2 cups sugar
1 quart hot water
1-gallon jar
4 teaspoons root-beer
extract

1. In small bowl, dissolve yeast in warm water.
2. In large bowl, dissolve sugar in hot water.
3. In gallon jar, mix contents of both bowls and root-beer extract.
4. Fill jar with warm water, stir, and cover.
5. Set jar in warm, sunny spot for 4 hours. Keep root beer covered until the following day, when it will be ready to drink.
6. Chill root beer before serving.

Makes 10 to 12 servings

Fresh Ginger Ale

*2 cups fresh ginger, peeled
and chopped
3 strips lemon peel
4 cups water
1 1/2 cups sugar
3 quarts chilled seltzer or club soda
Ice cubes*

1. Place ginger, lemon peel, and water in large saucepan. Bring to a boil and simmer uncovered for about 10 minutes.
2. Stir in sugar and boil for another 15 minutes or so, until the liquid is reduced to about 3 cups.
3. Pour syrup through a sieve and discard ginger and lemon peel.
4. Allow syrup to cool, then cover and chill for at least two hours.
5. To serve, fill tall glasses with ice cubes, pour about 1/4 cup syrup into each glass, and add 1 cup seltzer or club soda. Stir and sip!

Makes about 12 servings

Cherry-Lime Rickey

*Ice cubes
1 lime, quartered
8 ounces soda water
2 tablespoons cherry syrup
Maraschino cherries,
chopped (optional)*

1. Fill a tall glass with ice and squeeze juice from lime wedges into it.
2. Pour soda water over the ice, add the cherry syrup, and stir. For extra flavor, mix the chopped cherries into the rickey.

VARIATIONS: Substitute lemon or orange for the lime; add strawberry or raspberry syrup instead of cherry.

Makes 1 serving

Roadside Lemonade Stand

Most of us remember the thrill we had the very first time we earned pocket money. As any successful entrepreneur knows, the secret to earning your own hard, cold cash lies in seeking out opportunities that fulfill a need in the community. On a hot summer day, you can count on people getting thirsty—meaning that, if you have a roadside lemonade stand, chances are very good that people will stop to drink. Here are some tried-and-true lemonade-stand secrets that you and your grandchildren can use to increase business and add more coins to the piggy bank.

MAKE A STAND

The more professional your operation looks, the more likely people will be to stop and taste your wares. Setting up a table, booth, or stand with an umbrella will attract more customers than simply sitting in a lawn chair next to a cooler. Try these simple ideas:

■ Stack a wooden plank or old bookshelf on top of milk crates or cinder blocks. Cover with a decorative picnic-style tablecloth, or paint, stencil, or decorate the plank. Shelves make perfect areas for cups, napkins, a cooler, and your cash box.

■ Create a canopy for a small wooden table. You'll need four $3^{1}/_{2}$- to 4-foot-long laths or similar wood strips (which can be purchased at a hardware store), a drill, some screws, tacks, strong flexible wire, and enough fabric to drape over the frame. Fasten a lath firmly to each table leg with two screws so that it sticks up above the table and doesn't rotate. Place a tack in the top of each lath and stretch the wire around the tacks to connect the four poles. Drape the fabric over the frame and use additional tacks to secure it in place.

ADVERTISE

Let people know where you are and what you're selling.

- Use colorful sidewalk chalk to draw arrows several blocks away in every direction and point people your way.
- Make signs on poster board that you can attach to nearby telephone poles or lampposts.
- Make a sandwich board advertising your location and have your partner wear it at a corner of a busy intersection.

PICK YOUR SPOT

Location can be everything. Think ahead to make your lemonade spot work for you.

- Set up your stand where there will be heavy pedestrian traffic.
- If there are bicyclists in your area, avoid being on a significant slope—peddlers may not want to stop in the middle of an uphill climb or downhill coast.
- Put your stand near a shady tree or grassy area to encourage folks to sip in the shade and cool off.

QUALITY QUENCHERS

The first drink might be easy to sell, but you'll get repeat customers with fresh ingredients.

- Set a bowl of fresh lemons, limes, and oranges on your stand. It'll let people know they're getting real juice.
- Don't dilute. Keep a separate cooler for ice and wait until you get an order before pouring lemonade over ice.
- Offer a variety. Keep bottles of club soda or seltzer on hand to make lemonade spritzers. For some failsafe recipes, try Old-time Quenchers, page 206.

Jokes Food

What did the mother ghost tell the baby ghost when he ate too fast?

Stop goblin your food.

How many sandwiches can you eat on an empty stomach?

One. After the first, your stomach is no longer empty

What two things are never eaten for breakfast?

Lunch and dinner.

Why did the orange stop?

Because it ran out of juice.

Why did the student eat his homework?

The teacher told him it was a piece of cake.

What's the worst thing about being an octopus?

Washing your hands before dinner.

What starts with a "t," ends with a "t," and is full of "t"?

A teapot

When do you stop at green, and go at red?

When you're eating a watermelon

How do you make an egg laugh?

Tell it a yolk.

HERE IN BRAND-NEW HAT AND TIE-
IS MISTER JAKE McPHLISTER.

TURN THE PICTURE ROUND ABOUT
AND SEE HIS CHARMING SISTER!

Tommy Tucker's Pets

Y ou know Mother Goose's little boy named Tommy Tucker who sang for his supper. He was very fond of pets. He had a red hen, a white duck, a brown pig, and a black dog. Every day Tommy gave his pets their supper. He gave his red hen and his white duck some corn. He gave his little brown pig some milk; and he gave his black dog a bone with meat on it.

One afternoon Tommy Tucker played and played. He was very tired when he came into the house for his supper. He was so tired that he forgot all about his pets.

Red Hen, White Duck, Brown Pig, and Black Dog waited and waited and waited for Tommy Tucker to come and give them their supper. But Tommy did not.

"Cluck, cluck," said Red Hen. "I am hungry. Little Tommy Tucker didn't give me my supper. I shall find him." And away she went.

On the way she met White Duck. "Where are you going, Red Hen?" asked White Duck.

"Little Tommy Tucker didn't give me my supper," answered Red Hen. "I am going to find him. Cluck, cluck!"

"Little Tommy Tucker didn't give me *my* supper," said White Duck. "I will go with you. Quack, quack!" And she followed Red Hen.

Before long they met Brown Pig. "Where are you going, Red Hen and White Duck?" asked Brown Pig.

And they answered, "Little Tommy Tucker didn't give us our supper. We are going to find him."

"Little Tommy Tucker didn't give me *my* supper. I will go with you. Grunt, grunt!" said Brown Pig. And he followed Red Hen and White Duck.

When they came near the porch of Little Tommy Tucker's house they met Tommy Tucker's dog.

"Bow-wow!" he said. "Where are you going, Red Hen, White Duck,

214

Tommy Tucker's Pets

and Brown Pig?"

And they answered, "Little Tommy Tucker didn't give us our supper. We are going to find him."

"He didn't give me *my* supper," said Black Dog. "I will go with you. Bow-wow-wow."

And he followed Red Hen, White Duck, and Brown Pig.

When they reached the porch of Tommy Tucker's house, whom do you think they saw? There was Tommy Tucker fast asleep. Red Hen called out, "There is Tommy Tucker. He is fast asleep."

Then they all stood in a row and looked at Tommy.

"Little Tommy Tucker sings for his supper. We will sing for ours."

Then they all began:
"Cluck, cluck, cluck,
Quack, quack, quack!
Grunt, grunt, grunt!
Bow-wow, Bow-wow, Bow-wow!

Their song wakened Little Tommy Tucker. Up he jumped, for he remembered that he hadn't given them any supper.

"My little pets, you are singing for your supper," said Tommy Tucker. And away he ran to get it for them.

He fed Red Hen and White Duck with plenty of corn. He gave Brown Pig a big pan of milk, and he brought Black Dog a *nice* bone with some meat on it.

After his pets had finished eating Little Tommy Tucker heard, "Cluck, cluck! Quack, quack! Grunt, Grunt! Bow-wow!"

You know what they were trying to say to Tommy Tucker because he had given them their supper.

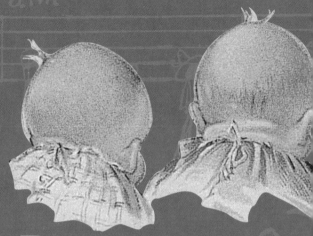

Do your ears hang low?
Do they wobble to and fro?
Can you tie them in a knot?
Can you tie them in a bow?
Can you throw them over your shoulder
  like a Continental soldier?
Do your ears hang low?

Do your ears hang high?
Do they reach up to the sky?
Do they droop when they're wet?
Do they stiffen when they're dry?
Can you semaphore your neighbor
  with a minimum of labor?
Do your ears hang high?

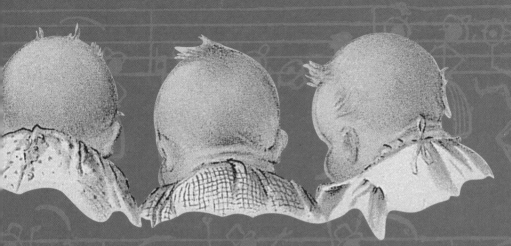

Do your ears hang wide?
Do they flap from side to side?
Do they wave in the breeze?
From the slightest little sneeze?
Can you soar above the nation with
    a feeling of elation?
Do your ears hang wide?

Do your ears fall off?
When you give a great big cough?
Do they lie there on the ground?
Or bounce up at every sound?
Can you stick them in your pocket
    just like little Davy Crockett?
Do your ears fall off?

Do Your Ears Hang Low?

ACTIVITIES

Peanut Pals

Peanuts are a delicious and healthy snack you can find in almost any household. These clever little peanut toys are sure to put a smile on your grandchild's face! Peanut-shell finger buddies are a snap to create and can be decorated a million different ways. And peanut pets are adorable mini-friends that can keep kids busy for an entire afternoon. Try putting on a peanut puppet show or peanut circus!

PEANUT FINGER BUDDIES

Shell some large peanuts by breaking the shells in half crosswise. Put an empty half-shell on the tip of a finger and draw a face on it with crayons or markers. Cover all fingers with peanut-shell faces, and have them talk to each other. It's a peanut-buddy party! You can even sew on hats or hair using a large needle and thread and bits of fabric, ribbon, or yarn. Or leave a peanut whole and draw a face on the shell. Then make a stand for the peanut by joining the ends of a strip of paper to make a ring that is slightly smaller than the peanut. Prop up the nut inside.

PEANUT PETS

■ Make a charming peanut puppy from a whole peanut in the shell by making two small holes at each end of the shell and inserting four matchsticks for legs. Add a short matchstick for a tail. Decorate the shell by drawing on a nose, eyes, and mouth with markers, and glue on two ears made from tiny pieces of paper. Or create a lovable lion. For the mane, cut a circle out of fabric, fringe the outer edge with scissors, and cut a small hole in the middle for the peanut to fit through. Alternatively, simply fringe the edge of a strip of paper and join the ends to make a ring. For the tail, color a small bit of cotton from a cotton ball yellow, and glue it to the end of the matchstick tail.

■ A peanut in the shell is also the perfect shape for making a cuddly little bunny. Prop a large peanut up on one end, draw eyes, nose, mouth, and whiskers with marker or crayon, and glue on two long ears made from paper. Don't forget to glue some cotton from a cotton ball to his back to make his tail!

■ Create a wise old owl by standing a peanut up on its large end and propping it in a stand or a little bit of modeling clay. Draw on a face using markers or crayons, and glue on ears and wings made of bits of feathers or shredded paper.

TEN LITTLE PUPPY DOGS

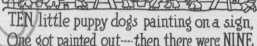

TEN little puppy dogs painting on a sign,
One got painted out----then there were NINE.

NINE little puppy dogs writing on a slate,
One was subtracted--- then there were EIGHT.

EIGHT little puppy dogs playing "odd and even,"
One got counted out---then there were SEVEN.

SEVEN little puppy dogs playing circus tricks,
One barked himself away-- then there were SIX.

SIX little puppy dogs playing with a hive,
Busy bees drove one off---then there were FIVE.

FIVE little puppy dogs going to the store,
One lost his little self---then there were FOUR.

FOUR little puppy dogs sailing o'er the sea,
One swam away to shore---then there were THREE.

THREE little puppy dogs bought a pot of glue,
One got stuck to a pig---then there were TWO.

TWO little puppy dogs snoozing in the sun,
One dreamed he was a bone---then there was ONE.

ONE little puppy dog hunting for a penny,
He got lost himself --- then there wasn't ANY!

What Frightened Peter Rabbit

One bright morning when Peter Rabbit was eating sweet clover in the field something jumped up in front of him. It was big and black and it had two long ears. Wasn't Peter Rabbit frightened! He hopped away as fast as he could go.

He was hurrying along when he met Bushy Squirrel.

"Why are you hopping away so fast, Peter?" asked Bushy.

"O Bushy," said Peter, "when I was eating sweet clover in the field this morning something frightened me."

"Did you see it?" asked Bushy.

"I did," said Peter.

"What did it look like, Peter?"

"It was big and black and it had two long ears. When I hopped it hopped. Can you tell me what it was?"

Bushy Squirrel thought for a moment. Then he said, "Indeed I cannot, Peter. Let us find Brown Hare. He will know what it was that frightened you, I'm sure."

Away went Peter Rabbit and Bushy Squirrel as fast as they could go. When they reached the woods Brown Hare saw them coming.

"Where are you going so fast, Bushy and Peter?" Brown Hare called out.

"O Brown Hare," said Peter, "I am so frightened. I am running away."

"What is the matter?" asked Brown Hare.

"This morning when I was eating sweet clover in the field something frightened me," said Peter.

"Did you see it?" asked Brown Hare.

"I did," said Peter.

"He did," said Bushy.

"What did it look like, Peter?"

"It was big and black," answered Peter.

"It was," said Bushy Squirrel.

"And it had two long ears," Peter added.

222

What Frightened Peter Rabbit

"It had," said Bushy Squirrel.

"Can you tell me what it was, Brown Hare?" asked Peter.

Brown Hare thought for a while; then he said slowly, "I cannot tell you, Peter Rabbit. Let us go and ask Wise Owl about it."

"We will," said Peter and Bushy.

Away went Peter Rabbit, Bushy Squirrel, and Brown Hare. They soon came to Wise Owl's home in the tree.

"Whoo-oo-who," called out Wise Owl.

"Peter Rabbit, Bushy Squirrel, and Brown Hare," answered the three.

"Why do you come to my tree when it is my bedtime?" asked Wish Owl in a very stern voice.

"O Wise Owl," said Peter Rabbit, "this morning when I was eating sweet clover in the field something frightened me."

"It did," said Bushy.

"Yes, it did," said Brown Hare.

"Did you see it, Peter?" asked Wise Owl then.

"Yes, I saw it," said Peter.

What Frightened Peter Rabbit

"He did," added Bushy.

"He certainly did," said Brown Hare.

"Tell me what it looked like, Peter," said Wise Owl.

"It was big and black."

"It was," said Bushy.

"It certainly was," added Brown Hare.

"And it had two long ears," Peter went on.

"It had," said Bushy.

"It certainly had," added Brown Hare.

"We have come to ask you what it was," said Peter Rabbit. "Can you tell us?"

Wise Owl put on his glasses and thought for a moment. Then he asked slowly, "You said you were in the field this morning?"

"I was," said Peter.

"He was," said Bushy Squirrel and Brown Hare.

"Was the sun shining, Peter?" asked Wise Owl.

"It was," answered Peter.

"It was," said Bushy Squirrel and Brown Hare.

Then Wise Owl thought again. Soon he burst out laughing and called to Peter, "Run out there in the sunshine, Peter, and turn round and round and round."

Peter Rabbit did as Wise Owl told him to do. As he turned round something jumped in front of him. It was big and black, and it had two long ears. When Peter hopped, it hopped.

"Ha, ha, ha!" laughed Peter. "I was afraid of my own shadow!"

"Your own shadow," said Bushy Squirrel in surprise.

"Afraid of your own shadow," called out Brown Hare in surprise.

Then they all laughed and laughed and laughed.

"Thank you, Wise Owl," said Peter. "I will go back to the field and eat sweet clover."

"Never be afraid of shadows," called out Wise Owl, as Peter Rabbit and Bushy Squirrel and Brown Hare hopped and frisked away.

How Many Seconds?

BY CHRISTINA ROSSETTI

How many seconds in a minute?
Sixty, and no more in it.

How many minutes in an hour?
Sixty for sun and shower.

How many hours in a day?
Twenty-four for work and play.

How many days in a week?
Seven both to hear and speak.

How many weeks in a month?
Four, as the swift moon runn'th.

How many months in a year?
Twelve the almanack makes clear.

How many years in an age?
One hundred says the sage.

How many ages in time?
No one knows the rhyme.

A TREE GROWS IN BROOKLYN
by Betty Smith

April 6, 1917.

The one-word headline was six inches high. The three letters were smudged at the edges and the word, WAR, seemed to waver.

Francie had a vision. Fifty years from now, she'd be telling her grandchildren how she had come to the office, sat at her reader's desk and in the routine of work had read that war had been declared. She knew from listening to her grandmother that old age was made up of such remembrances of youth.

But she didn't want to recall things. She wanted to live things—or as a compromise, re-live rather than reminisce.

She decided to fix this time in her life exactly the way it was this instant. Perhaps that way she could hold on to it as a living thing and not have it become something called a memory. . . .

Using the razor blade, she clipped a lock of her hair, wrapped it in the square of paper on which were her finger prints and lipstick mark, folded, it, placed it in the envelope and sealed the envelope. Then on the outside she wrote:

Frances Nolan, age 15 years and 4 months. April 6, 1917.

She thought: "If I open this envelope fifty years from now, I will be again as

I am now and there will be no being old for me. There's a long, long time yet before fifty years . . . millions of hours of time. But one hour has gone already since I sat here . . . one hour less to live . . . one hour gone away from all the hours of my life.

"Dear God," she prayed, "let me be *something* every minute of every hour of life. Let me be gay, let me be sad. Let me be cold; let me be warm. Let me be hungry . . . have too much to eat. Let me be ragged or well dressed. Let me be sincere—be deceitful. Let me be truthful; let me be a liar. Let me be honorable and let me sin. Only let me be *something* every blessed minute. And when I sleep, let me dream all the time so that not one little piece of living is ever lost."

Undercover Book Vault

*N*ever judge a book by its cover, the old adage goes. That couldn't be truer than with this crafty project, which turns an old hardcover into a secret storage box. Pick out the perfect hardcover book for a vault with your grandchildren. Younger grandchildren will delight in watching the transformation. Older grandchildren can help measure and glue the box frame.

Large, sturdy hardcover book at least 2" in thickness (the bigger and stronger, the better), measuring tape or ruler, pencil, scissors, X-acto knife, cardboard, glue

1. Open the book you plan to transform and turn a few pages past the title page. (These are the pages that you'll leave in the book.) The right-hand page is the one that you will cut. Using a ruler and pencil, draw a rectangle on that page. Leave a border of about one-inch from the drawn line to each edge of the page.

2. Measure the rectangle that you drew. Then measure the thickness of the book's interior pages. These dimensions will make up the volume of your book vault.

3. Measure and cut four pieces of cardboard to create a frame that matches the dimensions of your book vault.

4. Using an X-acto knife, carefully cut out the interior rectangle of all the pages in the book (except for those first few pages). Be sure to leave the outer borders of the interior pages intact, so it still appears to be a regular book when closed.

5. Glue the last page of the book to the inside of the back cover of the book.

6. Set the cardboard frame along the interior edges of your book vault and glue the frame to the cut edges of the interior pages. Let dry.

7. Now, your grandchildren will have a secret compartment in which to store pencils, pens, and trinkets.

Who Has Seen the Wind?

BY CHRISTINA ROSSETTI

Who has seen the wind?
  Neither I nor you:
But when the leaves hand trembling,
  The wind is passing through.

Who has seen the wind?
  Neither you nor I:
But when the trees bow down their heads,
  The wind is passing by.

LEGENDARY TALL TALES: SALLY ANN THUNDER ANN WHIRLWIND MEETS HER MATCH

1 iving on the frontier was a very difficult life. People were always so busy hunting or farming or protecting themselves that there wasn't much time for fun. But every once in awhile, pioneers would polish themselves up and have a rip-roarin' barn dance. Boys and girls would often meet at these dances and fall in love— wedding bells wouldn't be too far behind.

Sally Ann Thunder Ann Whirlwind didn't give a hoot about wedding bells, however. As her name suggested, pretty Sally Ann was full of energy and spirit. She boasted she could outrun a jackrabbit, out-wit a fox, and outwrestle any man in town. Supposedly, Sally Ann's voice was so powerful that she once screamed the feathers off an eagle's head, and that's how the bald eagle came to be. But she could also be enchanting. Once she charmed the skin right off a bear one cold winter. She wore a bee's nest as a Sunday bonnet and could often be seen running with wolves through the woods.

It was during one such excursion in the woods that she came across a hilarious sight. A man had somehow gotten his head stuck between two closely growing tree trunks and could not free himself!

"What do you think you're doing?" she asked between giggles.

The man was in no mood for jokes and answered angrily, "What does it look like? I fell asleep beneath these trees and somehow got my head stuck. I think the raccoons are playing a trick on me." He tugged again at his head, but it was stuck fast. "Well, are you going to help me or just stand there like a silly fool?"

Sally Ann didn't like his tone, but agreed to help. Quickly she found two long snakes and tied them together. Then, looping one over a trunk, she pulled back with all her might until the tree bent enough for the man to remove his head.

The man dusted off his raccoon-skin hat and started to walk away.

"Didn't anyone teach you any manners?" Sally Ann called after him, but he had already disappeared.

When she got back to the village, everyone was very excited about the barn dance that night. Sally Ann loved dancing, but she despised the fact that every single boy in the village had requested her as a date. Couldn't she just go by herself and have a good time? Finally she declared to her mother, "The only man who will be my partner is the man who can outdance me at the party!" And she meant it. So Sally Ann showed up by herself, looking as beautiful and fresh as a wild rose.

The first boy to ask her to dance was confident Tim Palmer. He thought he'd have no trouble keeping up with Sally

Ann, but two fast jigs tuckered him out, and as soon as he stopped for a moment, another boy, John Walker, took his place. John only lasted two dances. After that, a string of boys danced with Sally Ann, but each gave up, until only Sally Ann was left, still looking fresh and not even out of breath. She was just about to request a drink, when a voice piped up next to her.

"Might I try my hand at a dance with you?" She looked over to see the man with the raccoon-skin hat that she had rescued that morning.

"Oh, I see you suddenly learned some manners." She sniffed.

The man gave a sheepish grin. "Pardon me for this morning, miss. I was so embarrassed by my predicament that I just couldn't bear facing such a lovely creature as yourself." He stuck out his hand, "Allow me to introduce myself. My name's Davy Crockett. And you must be the famous Sally Ann Thunder Ann Whirlwind."

Sally Ann was amazed. Davy Crockett was a famous frontiersman, and here he was, asking her for a dance! But she remembered how rude he'd been that morning, and decided not to go easy on him during the next jig.

"I accept, Mr. Crockett," she said, ignoring his hand. "Let's hope your dancing is better then your manners." *After all,* she thought, *what would a frontiersman know about dancing?*

But Sally Ann was in for the surprise of her life. Davy Crockett's feet moved so fast that they were practically a blur. She tried all of her most complicated steps, but Davy Crockett kept up with each one. One, two, three dances went by. She could see the sweat standing on his forehead, but Davy Crocket never stopped smiling and never stopped dancing.

"Had enough?" she managed to gasp.

"Why, I'm just getting started," he said.

They danced like dervishes through the entire night and even into the next day! People were so amazed by the spec-tacle that they forgot to go to sleep. Sally Ann knew she couldn't keep it up forever. Suddenly, her ankle twisted and she fell forward. Quick as a wink, Davy Crockett shot out an arm and caught her.

"You win!" she cried, knowing that she had finally met her match.

Davy smiled at her. "Good. One more jig, and I would've been a goner."

Sally Ann and Davy Crockett soon married. Sally Ann never quit being feisty, but whenever she acted a little too stubborn, Davy would take out a fiddle and play a little dance tune, to remind her how he bested her fair and square. And whenever Davy forgot his manners, Sally Ann would look for a pair of good strong trees to stick his head between.

"And maybe this time," she'd laughingly tell him, "There won't be any snakes around to save you!" 🏃

As I was walking down the street,
Down the street, down the street,
A pretty girl I chanced to meet
Under the silv'ry moon.

Chorus
Buffalo gals, won't you come out tonight
Come out tonight, come out tonight.
Buffalo gals, won't you come out tonight
And dance by the light of the moon.

I asked her if she'd stop and talk,
Stop and talk, stop and talk.
Her feet took up the whole sidewalk;
She was fair to view.

Chorus

I asked her if she'd be my wife,
Be my wife, be my wife.
Then I'd be happy all my life
If she'd marry me.

Chorus

Buffalo Gals

HERE'S A GENTLE MOOLY COW
BY AN UPRIGHT LOG

TURN THE PICTURE ROUND LIKE THIS
AND FIND A FUNNY FROG

240

Jokes Animal

What time is it when an elephant sits on a fence?

Time to fix the fence.

How do you keep an elephant from charging?

Take away his credit card.

How do porcupines play leap-frog?

Very carefully!

Who says "quick, quick"?

A duck with the hiccups.

What did the pony say when he coughed?

"Pardon me, I'm a little horse."

What's the difference between a flea and a coyote?

One prowls on the hairy, the other howls on the prairie.

Why do they put bells on cows?

Because their horns don't blow.

Why was the baby ant so confused?

Because all of his uncles were ants.

What's the best way to catch a squirrel?

Climb a tree and act like a nut.

241

The Two Goats on The Bridge

Two goats that were each trying to cross a stream met in the middle of the bridge. The bridge wasn't wide enough for either goat to pass the other, so one said, "This plank won't hold us both. Let me by and then you can go on your way." But the other replied, "Why should I move? Why don't you step off the bridge and let me pass?" They argued like this for an hour, each one not letting the other pass, until finally they began pushing and fighting. Suddenly, the plank broke and both of the goats fell into the freezing water.

Moral: Don't be as stubborn as goats!

HEIDI

by Johanna Spyri

Where shall I sleep, Grandfather?"

"Wherever you like," he replied.

This was quite to Heidi's way of thinking. She looked into every nook and corner to see where would be the best place for her to sleep. In the corner by her grandfather's bed stood a little ladder, which led to the hayloft. Heidi climbed this. There lay a fresh, fragrant heap of hay, and through a round window one could look far down into the valley below.

"This is where I want to sleep," Heidi called down. "It is lovely! Just come and see how lovely it is up here, Grandfather!"

"I know all about it," sounded from below.

"I am going to make a bed," called out the child again as she ran busily to and fro in the loft. "But you must come up here and bring a sheet, for the bed must have a sheet to lie on."

"Well, well," said the grandfather below; and after a few moments he went to the cupboard and rummaged about; then he drew out from under his shirts a long, coarse piece of cloth, which might serve for a sheet. He came up the ladder and found that a very net little bed had been made in the hayloft; the hay was piled up

HEIDI

higher at one end to form the pillow, and the bed was placed in such a way that one could look from it straight out through the round open window.

"That is made very nicely," said the grandfather. "Next comes the sheet; but wait a moment"—and he took up a good armful of hay and made the bed twice as thick, in order that the hard floor might not be felt through it. "There, now put it on."

Heidi quickly took hold of the sheet, but was unable to lift it, it was so heavy; however, this made it all the better because the sharp wisps of hay could not push through the firm cloth. Then the two together spread the sheet over the hay, and where it was too broad or too long Heidi quickly tucked it under. Now it appeared quite trim and neat, and Heidi stood looking at it thoughtfully.

"We have forgotten one thing, Grandfather," she said.

"What is that?" he asked.

"The blanket; when we go to bed we creep in between the sheet and the blanket."

"Is that so? But if I haven't any?" asked the old man.

"Oh, then it's no matter." said Heidi soothingly. "We can take more hay for a blanket." She was about to run to the haystack again, but her grandfather prevented her.

"Wait a moment," he said, and went down the ladder to his own bed. Then he came back and laid a large, heavy linen sack on the floor.

"Isn't that better than hay?" he asked. Heidi pulled at the sack with all her

246

might and main, trying to unfold it, but her little hands could not manage the heavy thing. Her grandfather helped, and when it was finally spread out on the bed, it all looked very neat and comfortable.

Heidi, looking at her new resting place admiringly, said, "That is a splendid blanket, and the whole bed is lovely! How I wish it were night so that I could lie down in it!"

"I think we might have something to eat first," said the grandfather. "What do you think?"

In her excitement over the bed, Heidi had forgotten everything else; but now that eating was suggested to her, a great feeling of hunger rose within her, for she had taken nothing all day except a piece of bread and a few sips of weak coffee early in the morning, and afterward she had made the long journey. So Heidi heartily agreed, saying, "Yes, I think so too."

"Well, let us go down, since we are agreed," said the old man and followed close upon the child's steps. He went to the fireplace, pushed the large kettle aside and drew forward the little one that hung on the chain, sat down on the three-legged wooden stool with the round seat and kindled a bright fire. Almost immediately the kettle began to boil, and the old man held over the fire a large piece of cheese on the end of a long iron fork. He moved it this way and that, until it was golden yellow on all sides. Heidi looked on with eager attention. Suddenly a new idea came to her mind; she jumped up and ran to the cupboard, and kept going back and forth. When the grandfather brought the toasted cheese to the table, it was already nicely laid with the round loaf of bread, two plates, and two knives, for Heidi had noticed everything in the cupboard, and knew that all would be needed for the meal.

"That is right, to think of doing something yourself," said the grandfather, laying the cheese on the bread and putting the teapot on the table. "but there is still something missing from the table."

Heidi saw how invitingly the steam came out of the pot, and ran quickly back to the cupboard. But there was only one little bowl there. Heidi was not long puzzled; behind it stood two glasses; the child immediately came back with the bowl and a glass and placed them on the table.

"Very good. You know how to help yourself; but where are you going to sit?"

The grandfather himself was sitting in the only chair. Heidi shot like an arrow to the fireplace, brought back the little three-legged stool and sat down on it.

"Well, you have a seat, sure enough, only it is rather low," said the grandfather. "But in my chair also you would be too short to reach the table; still you must have something anyway, so come!"

Saying which he rose, filled the little bowl with milk, placed it on the chair, and pushed it close to the three-legged stool, so that Heidi had a table in front of her. The grandfather laid a large slice of bread and a piece of the golden cheese on the chair and said, "Now eat!"

He seated himself on the corner of the table and began his dinner. Heidi grasped her bowl and drank and drank without stopping, for all the thirst of her long journey came back to her. Then she drew a long breath and set down the bowl.

"Do you like the milk?" asked the grandfather.

"I never tasted such good milk before," answered Heidi.

"Then you must have some more." The grandfather filled the bowl again to the brim and placed it before the child, who looked quite content as she began to eat her bread, after it had been spread with the toasted cheese soft as butter. The combination tasted very good and in between bites she drank her milk and looked very content.

When the meal was over, the grandfather went out to the goat shed to put it in order, and Heidi watched him closely as he first swept it clean with a broom and then laid down fresh straw for the animals to sleep on. Then he went to his little workshop, cut some round sticks, shaped a board, made some holes in it, put the round sticks into them, and suddenly it was a stool like his own, only much higher. Heidi was speechless with amazement as she saw his work.

"What is this, Heidi?" asked the grandfather.

"It is a stool for me, because it is so high; you made it just like that!" said the child, still deeply astonished.

HEIDI

She knows what she sees; her eyes are in the right place, remarked the grandfather to himself as he went around the hut driving a nail here and there; then he repaired something in the door, and went from place to place with hammer, nails, and pieces of wood, mending or trimming away wherever it was needed. Heidi followed him step by step and watched him with the closest attention, and everything he did was very interesting to her.

Evening was coming on. It was beginning to blow harder in the old fir trees, for a mighty wind had sprung up and was whistling and moaning through their dense crowns. It sounded so beautiful in Heidi's ears and heart that she was quite delighted, and skipped and jumped under the firs as if she were experiencing the greatest pleasure of her life. The grandfather stood in the doorway and watched the child.

A shrill whistle sounded. Heidi stopped her jumping, and the grandfather stepped outside. Goat after goat came leaping down from above, like a pack of hounds, and Peter was in the midst of them. With a shout of joy Heidi rushed in among the flock and greeted her old friends of the morning one after the other.

When they reached the hut, they all stood still, and two pretty, slender goats—one white, the other brown—came out from the others to the grandfather and licked his hands, in which he held some salt to welcome them, as he did every evening. Peter disappeared with his flock. Heidi gently stroked first one goat and then the other and ran around them to stroke them on the other side; she was perfectly delighted with the little creatures.

HEIDI

"Are they ours, Grandfather? Are they both ours? Will they go into the shed? Will they stay with us always?" asked Heidi, one question following the other in her delight.

When the goats had finished licking their salt, the old man said, "Go and bring out your little bowl and the bread."

Heidi obeyed, and came back at once. The grandfather milked the goat and filled the bowl and cut off a piece of bread, saying, "Now eat your supper and then go up to bed! Your Aunt Dete left a bundle for you; your nightgowns and other things are in it. You will find it downstairs in the closet if you need it. I must attend to the goats now; so sleep well!"

"Good night, Grandfather! Good night—what are their names, Grandfather? What are their names?" cried the child, running after the old man and the goats as they disappeared into the shed.

"The white one is named Schwänli and the brown one Bärli," answered the grandfather.

"Good night, Schwänli! Good night Bärli!" called Heidi at the top of her voice. Then Heidi sat down on the bench and ate her bread and drank her milk; but the strong wind almost blew her off her seat; so she finished hastily, then went in and climbed up to her bed, in which she immediately fell asleep and slept as soundly and well as if she had been in the finest bed of a royal princess. ✗

Papa's Pasta Secrets

When cooking pasta, it's easy to plan ahead for fast-food dining. Just toss an extra serving or two of noodles into the pot. Once the pasta is cooked and drained, store the extra noodles in an airtight container. Stir the pasta with a bit of oil to prevent the noodles from sticking, then refrigerate. No cooking necessary for tomorrow's lunch or dinner: Just heat up the leftover pasta and sauce, and call it a meal.

String Pie

1 pound ground beef,
$1/2$ cup finely chopped onion
$1/4$ cup green pepper, diced
16 ounces favorite pasta sauce
8 ounces spaghetti, cooked
and drained
$1/3$ cup grated Parmesan cheese
2 eggs, beaten
1 tablespoon softened butter
1 cup cottage cheese
$1/2$ cup shredded mozzarella cheese

1. Preheat oven to 350°F.
2. In large skillet, cook beef, onion, and green pepper until meat is completely browned. Drain excess fat. Stir in pasta sauce.
3. In large bowl, combine pasta, Parmesan cheese, eggs, and butter until thoroughly mixed.
4. Transfer noodle mixture to 9- x 13-inch baking dish. Spread cottage cheese evenly over the top. Cover with sauce. Sprinkle top with mozzarella cheese.
5. Bake for 20 minutes, or until pie is heated through and cheese is melted.

Makes 6 servings

Fettuccine Alfredo

3/4 pound fettuccine
5 tablespoons butter
2/3 cup whipping cream
1/4 teaspoon salt,
Dash white pepper
Dash nutmeg
1 cup grated Parmesan cheese
2 tablespoons chopped fresh parsley

1. Cook pasta and set aside in large saucepan.
2. In a heavy skillet over medium heat, warm up butter and cream until bubbling. Stir for 2 minutes, then stir in salt, pepper, and nutmeg. Remove from heat.
3. Stir cheese into mixture until sauce is smooth.
4. Pour sauce over noodles. Toss over low heat for 2 to 3 minutes until fettuccine is thoroughly coated and sauce is thickened.
5. Serve with fresh parsley on top.

Makes 4 servings

No-Fuss Ravioli-Spinach Lasagna

Nonstick vegetable spray
1 (26-ounce) jar pasta sauce
1 (30-ounce) package of frozen cheese ravioli
1 (10-ounce) package of frozen spinach, thawed and squeezed dry
8 ounces shredded mozzarella cheese
1/2 cup grated Parmesan cheese

1. Preheat oven to 350°F.
2. Coat a 9- x 13-inch baking pan with cooking spray.
3. Spoon a third of the sauce into pan, then layer half the ravioli and all the spinach on top. Add half the mozzarella and half the Parmesan cheese. Top with the remaining ravioli, sauce, and cheese.
4. Cover pan with aluminum foil and bake for 25 minutes.
5. Remove foil and bake for an additional 5 to 10 minutes, or until cheese is bubbly.

Makes 6 servings

Still Here

BY LANGSTON HUGHES

I've been scared and battered.

My hopes the wind done scattered.

Snow has friz me, sun has baked me.

Looks like between 'em

They done tried to make me

Stop laughin', stop lovin', stop livin'—

But I don't care!

I'm still here!

Br'er Rabbit Outfoxes Br'er Fox

A long time ago, animals acted very differently from the way they do today. They could speak to each other, lived in cottages, and even wore clothes! And the animal who was most proud of his bright home and smart wardrobe was clever Br'er Rabbit. Br'er was a term that meant "brother" and all the animals called each other that because they thought of themselves as one big family.

Br'er Rabbit liked to wear a pair of clean overalls and a big, wide-brimmed hat that he had cut two holes out of so his ears could poke through. He even went so far as to stick a watch attached to a beautiful gold chain into his front pocket!

He lived in a little house that was right next to a big patch of thorny bushes and brambles. It was a secret hideout, because the thorny bushes camouflaged the ground underneath, which was soft and sandy and an excellent place to take a nap.

Br'er Rabbit was quick and clever, and this sometimes got him into trouble. He thought he was so smart that he often snubbed other animals or played tricks on them. Life in the woods was dangerous at times, but overall, it was a friendly place to live. Although the other animals didn't enjoy Br'er Rabbit's tricks, they usually just grumbled and went about their business.

All the animals, that is, except for Br'er Fox. Now, even though the rest of the animals called him "Br'er," they certainly didn't feel very comfortable including him in their family! Br'er Fox was lean and strong, and he was so crafty, it was said he could talk the feathers off a sparrow. He had had his eye on Br'er Rabbit from the first day he moved into the woods. Never had he seen such a plump and juicy rabbit, and he

couldn't wait to make him into a delicious stew, or barbecue him over a roaring fire!

Br'er Rabbit during this time acted very foolishly. Instead of being careful and keeping a good watch on the cunning Fox, Br'er Rabbit merely ignored him. "It'll take more than some dirty, mangy fox to get old Br'er Rabbit in the pot!" he told his friends.

The wily Fox knew that Br'er Rabbit was a clever fellow, so he bided his time until he had figured out a very sneaky plan.

In one corner of the woods was a murky swamp full of snakes, toads, and thick, sticky black mud. This mud was famous for being so sticky and gross that once it stuck to a bit of your clothes or your body, it would take days to wash off! Br'er Fox chuckled to himself as he gathered a big pail of the mud and took it back to his den. There, he created a little figure out of the mud that looked like a good-size rabbit. He even painted a face on it. Then he set the mud figure in the path that led to Br'er Rabbit's house and waited for the bunny to arrive.

It didn't take long before he heard Br'er Rabbit cheerfully whistling. He was on his way to a party at Br'er Chipmunk's house and he thought he looked especially good that afternoon.

"If there's a rabbit more good-looking then me, I've never met him!" he exclaimed, and then stopped short when he saw the mud figure in the middle of the path.

"Good afternoon, Br'er," he said, tipping his wide hat. "Don't suppose you'd mind if I just slipped past you down the path now, would you?"

The mud figure said nothing.

"Maybe he's hard of hearing," Br'er Rabbit thought. Leaning in close to the mud figure he yelled, "Hey, buddy, I'd like to get by."

But of course, the mud figure was silent.

Now, Br'er Rabbit started to get a little annoyed at this. "Listen, I've got somewhere to be. I'm on my way to a wild party where I'm sure they'll be plenty of girl rabbits to charm, so I need you to step aside."

Still, the mud figure would not answer him.

"All right, that's it," said Br'er Rabbit. "If you don't move on the count of three, I'm going to have to wallop you good. One...two...three!!!" Since the mud figure never moved, Br'er Rabbit brought back a paw and—WHACK!—slapped the mud figure right in the face!

But instead of getting the mud figure's attention, Br'er Rabbit's paw stuck fast!

"Let go of my paw, you cretin!" Br'er Rabbit bellowed. He swung the other paw. WHACK! This time it stuck to the mud figure's belly.

"What kind of trick is this?" He yelled, and then gathering all of his strength, he pulled back one of his long, strong legs and kicked the mud figure right in the shin! Imagine how surprised he was when he found that both arms and a leg were glued to the dark figure!

At this point, Br'er Rabbit heard a low chuckling coming from the bushes. Turning his head with difficulty, he saw Br'er Fox appear.

"Why Br'er Rabbit, looks like you are in a bit of a jam." He laughed.

"This isn't funny. Would you please help me get free?" Br'er Rabbit asked.

Br'er Fox merely laughed some more. "Now why would I want to do that?" He studied poor Br'er Rabbit, who was now covered in sticky mud. "I suppose I'll have to give you a good washing before I cook you."

Br'er Rabbit gulped, "You're going to eat me?"

"Of course," he answered, "Why do you think I set this trap? Now, should I slather you in BBQ sauce and grill you up? Or would you be

better in a thick, sumptuous soup? All that struggling might have made you tough and stringy."

Br'er Rabbit was frightened out of his wits and he tried to get away, but it was no use. The sticky mud had glued him to the spot! He thought quickly of a way to escape. Suddenly, he remembered the patch of thorns by his house.

"Oh, Br'er Fox, if you must eat me, then eat me. But please don't throw me in that patch of thorns!" he said, gesturing to the thorny brambles next to his house.

Br'er Fox looked at him strangely. "You know, that's not such a bad idea. It might tenderize you."

"Oh, no! That's the worst thing in the world! Anything, anything but the patch of thorns!"

Br'er Fox nodded and then gathered Br'er Rabbit up. "That's settled. I'll toss you in the thorns and then have myself a cookout!"

Br'er Rabbit struggled and begged not to be thrown in, but Br'er Fox didn't listen. With a

"heave, ho!" he tossed Br'er Rabbit right in the middle of the patch! He stood aside, chuckling, listening to Br'er Rabbit yelp and thrash around. Then suddenly the patch got quiet. Br'er Fox leaned forward to investigate and found the thorn patch empty! From up the path he heard the sound of laughter and turned to see Br'er Rabbit free and running away.

The rabbit called back over his shoulder. "Thanks for tossing me in. Those thorns really did a good job of scraping all that sticky mud off! Why, I probably would've ruined my best clothes if you hadn't!" Then he was gone.

Br'er Fox was so angry that his eyes shot sparks and the whole forest rang with his yells. But he knew that Br'er Rabbit had out-witted him.

And that's just one of the many times that cunning Br'er Rabbit proved he was the trickiest character in the entire woods! ☀

Savory Snacks

Nothing beats homemade snacks after school, after a soccer game, or during a movie on a rainy day. The treat can begin in the kitchen with simple and quick recipes that make it easy to introduce young grandchildren to cooking. Start by looking in your freezer, refrigerator, or pantry for ingredients you probably already have. From start to finish, these finger-licking snacks can be ready to eat in less than a half hour. Yum!

Down-home Potato Chips

2 medium-size red potatoes, scrubbed
2 tablespoons herbs or spices (such as dill, rosemary, dried onion flakes, or BBQ seasoning)
1/2 teaspoon garlic salt
1/4 teaspoon pepper
Nonstick cooking spray
1 tablespoon olive oil

1. Preheat oven to 450°F.
2. Slice potatoes very thin and pat dry with paper towels.
3. In small bowl, combine herbs, garlic salt, and pepper. Set aside.
3. Coat baking sheet with nonstick cooking spray and arrange potato slices in a single layer on the sheet.
4. Spray potato slices with cooking spray and bake 10 minutes.
5. Turn slices over and brush with oil. Sprinkle herb mixture evenly onto slices. Bake for 5 to 10 minutes longer, or until chips are golden brown.
6. Cool on baking sheet before serving.

Makes 4 to 6 servings

MENU
BALED HAY
HEADS of CABBAGE
MEADOW GRASS
CORN ON THE COB
RIPE APPLES
OATS IN ANY STYLE
SHELLED CORN

ICE CREAM

Bruschetta Bites

2 cloves garlic, minced
3 plum tomatoes, diced
$3/4$ cup olive oil
10 to 15 fresh basil leaves,
finely chopped
Salt and pepper to taste
1 baguette, cut in $1/2$-inch slices

1. In medium-size bowl, mix together garlic, tomatoes, oil, and basil. Stir in salt and pepper to taste. Set aside.
2. Heat 1 to 2 tablespoons olive oil in large skillet over medium heat. Grill baguette slices on both sides.
3. Top bread slices with tomato mixture and serve immediately.

Makes 4 to 6 servings

Dogs in Blankets

*8 hot dogs (veggie, beef, pork,
chicken, or turkey)*
8 thin slices cheese
1 (8-ounce) package crescent rolls
Mustard

1. Preheat oven to 375°F.
2. Cut a partial slit lengthwise
   down the middle of each hot dog
   and fill it with a slice of cheese.
3. Wrap each hot dog with a seg-
   ment of crescent dough roll.
4. Place hot dogs on a baking sheet
   and bake for about 12 minutes,
   or until rolls are golden brown.
5. Cut hot dogs into thirds and
   serve hot with mustard.

Makes 24 servings

Cheesy Chicken Nuggets

$1/2$ cup bread crumbs
$1/4$ teaspoon pepper
$1/4$ cup finely grated cheddar cheese

1 teaspoon dried basil
$1/2$ teaspoon salt
*4 boneless chicken breasts,
cut into bite-size pieces*
$1/2$ cup melted butter
*Barbecue sauce (or honey mustard
sauce or ranch dressing)*

1. Preheat oven to 400°F.
2. In large bowl, combine bread
   crumbs, pepper, cheddar cheese,
   basil, and salt, and mix until
   well blended.
3. Dip each chicken piece in the
   melted butter, then roll in the
   crumb mixture until coated.
4. Place nuggets on nonstick baking
   sheet and bake for 10 to 15 minutes, or until juices run clear
   when tested with a knife.
5. Serve with barbecue sauce, honey
   mustard sauce, or ranch dressing
   for dipping.

Makes 8 to 10 servings

The Oak & The Weeds

A mighty, proud oak tree was uprooted during a storm and fell into a brook. It floated downstream until it came to rest beside a patch of weeds. "Isn't that strange?" thought the oak. "These weeds are weak and small and yet they have survived the storm. I am a strong oak, and yet the storm has torn me up by the roots!" A weed that had heard the oak replied, "It is because you are so proud and stiff that you were blown down. We weeds bow and yield to the wind, and so we remain standing even after you have fallen."

Moral: Sometimes it is better to bend and be flexible than to remain stiff and stubborn.

The Boy & The Cookie Jar

A little boy reached into a cookie jar to grab some chocolate-chip cookies, which were his favorite. They looked so delicious that instead of just taking one, he grabbed a handful. But when he tried to pull his hand out, he realized that the opening was too small and his hand was stuck. Again and again he tried to pull the cookies up, but it was no use. He was about to start crying when his mother came in and saw his situation. "If you had only taken one, you could have pulled your hand out easily and would be munching on that cookie right now! Instead, you don't have any by trying to take too many at once," she told him.

Moral: It is better to have a little than none at all.

The Golden Goose

Once there was a man who had three sons. The youngest boy was given the nickname "Dummling" because his whole family thought he was very stupid and lazy.

One day, the oldest son decided to go into the forest to cut some wood. His mother packed him an excellent lunch, which included a thick, tasty sandwich and a big slice of cake, so he wouldn't be hungry. The boy set out, but had hardly made it into the forest before he encountered a small, gray-haired old man.

"Good day," said the old man. "I am very hungry. Would you perhaps share your lunch with me?"

The eldest son sneered. "If I give you my lunch, then I will hardly have enough for myself now, won't I?" he reasoned, and went on his way.

But just as he was about to cut down a tree, the ax slipped and the handle banged right on his foot, so he had to go home and have the injury taken care of.

A few days later, the second son wanted to go cut wood in the forest. Again, his mother packed him a wonderful lunch with a delicious sandwich and big piece of cake. And just like his brother, he met an old man.

"Good day," he said to the second son. "My stomach is so empty! Would you mind sharing your lunch with me?"

Now, the second son was even more selfish than the eldest was. "Whatever I give to you will be taken away from me!" he declared.

He continued on and had just found a tree to cut, when he slipped on a root and banged his head on a tree trunk, and so had to turn around and go home.

Then Dummling asked his father, "May I please go cut wood?"

The father snorted. "Look at what happened to your strong,

smart brothers! Do you think you'll do any better?"

But Dummling persisted, and finally they let him go. But all he got from his mother was two pieces of stale bread and a moldy apple.

When Dummling came to the forest, he also met the old man. "Good day," he greeted Dummling, "I am so hungry! Will you please share your lunch with me?"

"Of course," answered Dummling. "But I'm afraid all I have is a moldy apple and some stale bread." Yet, when he opened his bag, he found a whole stack of mouth-watering sandwiches and the sweetest, juiciest-looking pie he had ever seen. So, he and the old man ate a huge lunch, and afterward the old man said, "Because you have a generous heart, I will tell you a little secret. Underneath this very tree is a treasure. Cut it down and you will find something." Before Dummling could even thank him, the old man disappeared!

"How peculiar," thought Dummling. But he set to work cutting the tree down, and once it fell, he found a goose with feathers made of pure gold sitting among the roots. He knew if he took the golden goose back to his house, his family would probably steal it, so he decided to set out in the world and see what he could find on his own.

That night, Dummling stayed at an inn in a nearby town. When the innkeeper and his family saw him enter with the magical goose, they immediately made plans to snatch it. As soon as Dummling fell asleep, the innkeeper's eldest daughter crept into his room and went to grab it. Imagine her surprise when she was unable to pull her hand away no matter how hard she pulled! She struggled so much, that her mother crept in to see what was the matter. "Stop messing around and get that goose!" she hissed at the girl as she pulled her arm. And just like that, she was stuck to her daughter!

Both the mother and the daughter tried desperately to yank themselves away, but it was no use. The next morning, Dummling picked the goose up, not seeming to notice the two people trailing behind. As he made his way out the door, the innkeeper's youngest daughter saw the strange line of people and cried, "Mother, where are you going?" Before they could stop her, she plucked at her mother's dress, and was also forced to trot along after the golden goose!

As they made their way through the town, everyone who saw the three people trailing behind Dummling burst out laughing, they looked so foolish trying to keep up!

"Hey," one man called, "you should show the princess your golden goose!" The man told Dummling that in this town lived a princess who was so serious that she had never smiled once in her entire life. In fact, the king had decreed that anyone who could make her laugh could marry her.

Dummling made his way to the palace and walked before the princess with the golden goose and the innkeeper's family trotting along behind him. They all looked so strange that the princess immediately started laughing, and didn't stop until she had fallen off her royal throne and was rolling on the floor! The king knew this meant Dummling would want his daughter's hand in marriage, but he didn't like the idea of his only daughter marrying a commoner.

"I will let you marry my daughter," said the king, "but first you must bring me someone who can drink up an entire lake in one gulp!"

Dummling immediately thought of the little old man who had told him of the golden goose, and went to the woods to find him. When he got to the tree, he saw a man with a very sad face.

"What's the matter?" he asked.

"I have this terrible thirst! Nothing makes it go away, no

matter how much I drink! It's really terrible!" he exclaimed.

Dummling knew just what to do, and brought the man to a lake by the castle. With one giant gulp, the man emptied the entire lake and then patted his belly.

Now, instead of letting the princess marry Dummling, the king came up with another plan. "I have decided that you may only marry my daughter if you can show me a person hungry enough to eat a mountain of bread!"

Immediately, Dummling went back to the forest, and this time he found a woman who was crying.

"What's wrong?" asked Dummling.

"Oh, I'm always so hungry!" cried the woman. "Morning, noon, and night! I've eaten a whole oven full of rolls, and I'm still starving!"

"Come with me," said Dummling, and he led her to a giant mountain of bread that the king had had baked next to his castle. The woman immediately began stuffing her face, and before the day was through, she had eaten the whole thing!

When Dummling asked for his princess this time, the king said, "I've changed my mind. I will only let my daughter marry you if you can give me a ship that sails on water *or* land!"

Dummling was getting a little tired of all the king's orders, but again he went to the forest, and this time he met the little old man. He listened to what Dummling wanted, and then he said, "I will give you the ship, just as I provided the man who drank the lake and the woman who ate the mountain. And I'll do it all because of the kindness you showed me once."

So, Dummling sailed back to the castle on the ship that floated on water or land, and the princess didn't even give her father a chance to change his mind before accepting Dummling's marriage proposal.

Ship Ahoy!

S ummer is the ideal time to spend at the lake launching new boats in the water and seeing how they sail. Balsa wood, found at your local craft or hardware store, is perfect for such carving projects. Younger grandchildren can enjoy helping with the boat plans while granddad does the carving. Older grandchildren can hone their woodworking skills and enjoy watching their handiwork float along the shore.

Carving knife; 7" x 1^1/$_2$" x 2" balsa wood block (for the hull); ruler; drill with ^{3}/$_{16}$" bit; sandpaper; waterproof paint; super glue; 5^1/$_2$" x 6^1/$_2$" x 6^1/$_2$" triangle of water-resistant nylon cloth (sail); ^{3}/$_{16}$" diameter wooden dowel, 7^1/$_4$" long (mast); hammer (optional); nail (optional); silicone spray sealant

1. Using the carving knife, cut off 2 corners on the 2-inch side of the 7-inch block of balsa, so that it now looks like one side is pointed. This is the front of the boat, or "bow."

2. About 4 inches from the rear of the boat (or "stern,") drill a hole ^{1}/$_4$-inch deep for the mast.

3. Sand and paint the boat and allow to dry completely.

4. Glue the shorter side of the sail's triangle onto the mast. Insert a few drops of glue into the hole in the hull and insert the mast. Or attach the mast by hammering a short nail through the bottom of the boat up into the dowel.

5. Spray the finished boat with sealant, and allow to dry before setting sail.

A Fable by Aesop

The Blue Jay
& The Owl

One day, an old barn owl had a visit from his good friend, the blue jay. The owl sat quietly in a little corner while the blue jay talked about all the things he was doing and all of the other birds he had visited. In fact, the blue jay talked so much that the owl did not say a single word the entire time! After an hour of talking nonstop, the blue jay fluffed up his feathers and said goodbye. "Dear owl, I can't remember the last time I had such a wonderful conversation with someone! You've cheered me up so much!" he called as he flew away.

Moral: Sometimes all you need to do is sit still and listen.

The Cat, The Mouse
& The Rooster

One day a very young mouse came home and said, "I saw the most terrible thing in the garden! It strutted about on two legs and was as black as coal. It wore a red flag on its head, and a red scarf tied around its throat, and it flapped its arms up and down in a very alarming way. It stretched its neck out and roared at me until I thought it would eat me up! It made me shake from head to foot and I ran home as fast as I could!" The little mouse sighed. "And what's even worse was that I was just about to make friends with a very pretty creature! She had soft, dark fur like ours, and a long tail, and appeared so friendly that I'm positive we would have been good friends. She looked at me with her bright eyes and opened her mouth, and I'm sure she was about to speak to me when that horrible creature started raising a racket and I ran away!

An old mouse shook his head. "My dear child, the noisy creature you saw was only a rooster, and roosters have always gotten along with mice. But the pretty thing you were so fond of was a cat, and cats eat mice !"

Moral: Don't judge others by their appearance.

LEGENDARY TALL TALES: WILD BILL HICKOCK & CALAMITY JANE

two of the wildest, craziest, toughest characters in the Old West were Wild Bill Hickock and Calamity Jane. The fantastic tales told about them could fill an encyclopedia, and what makes them even more amazing is that this pair actually existed!

Wild Bill's real name was James Butler Hickock. He got his nickname from his wild antics and daring feats. Even as a young boy, people knew his life would be full of adventure. As a teenager, he became an expert marksman with a gun and held a number of strange and wonderful jobs. He was a canal driver, a scout, and even a spy for the Union Army during the Civil War.

Wild Bill hated wearing his stiff Sunday clothes as a child, and disliked it even more when he was a young man. Often times he would wear his clothes over and over again until they were filthy and people could smell him coming from a mile away.

One night, Wild Bill was driving a stagecoach across the frontier. It was getting late, so he decided to settle down and sleep beneath the stars. No sooner had he drifted off to sleep then he heard a strange snuffling sound coming from nearby. He cracked open his eyes. . . and saw a huge brown bear only five feet away from him!

Apparently, Wild Bill's clothing had smelled so strongly of bacon grease and other foods he had spilt on it that the bear had sniffed him out. Wild Bill lay absolutely still and watched the bear paw through his campground. He knew his guns were too far away to reach, and it was only a matter of time before the bear found him. The only thing he had to protect himself was his trusty knife. Quick as a flash, Wild Bill jumped up and ran at the bear. Even though it was surprised, the bear was ready for a fight. The ferocious bear clawed and bit Wild Bill again and again. Even with its razor-sharp claws and immense strength, the bear had met its match in Wild Bill. The battle was long and hard, but finally Wild Bill overcame the mighty bear using only his wits and his knife. After the battle, he struggled home to nurse his many wounds. Amazed people couldn't believe this wild story, and his reputation only grew bigger.

His strange adventures didn't end there. Even though Wild Bill loved to raise a ruckus and was known to be a big-time gambler, he was named U.S. Marshal of several rough Western towns. He was involved in many shoot-outs and single-handedly bested the McCanles gang—which contained more than ten men! He even grew his hair long as a challenge to the hostile Native Americans who scalped people they fought on the frontier. It seemed like there was no one who cast a bigger shadow in the American West than Wild Bill Hickock . . . until he came to Deadwood, South Dakota and met Calamity Jane.

Calamity Jane was born Martha Jane Cannary, and she was raised in an army camp. Being orphaned at a young age, she learned how to take care of herself and shoot, fight, and ride a

horse as well as the best cowboy. Not many jobs were available to women, but that didn't stop Calamity Jane from trying her hand at a number of occupations, most times dressing herself like a boy. She was even a Pony Express rider and braved the treacherous trails to bring messages from town to town. On one occasion, she saved a stagecoach that was being attacked by Native Americans by taking control of the horses when the driver was injured.

When Wild Bill Hickock and Calamity Jane got together in Deadwood, they raised enough noise to wake the dead! Deadwood was a notoriously rough town, but Wild Bill and Calamity Jane were surely the wildest of any of the cowboys. If they weren't racing through town on swift horses, they were whooping it up in the local saloons, or having a grand time at one of their many card games. They competed against each other over any little bet, and were constantly daring each other to do more outrageous and dangerous acts. The two were quite a pair, and some even thought they had been secretly married, although this was never proven.

Wild Bill Hickock later joined up with Buffalo Bill's Wild West Show as an expert shooter. He visited the whole country and met many different people. Unfortunately, he also got into many fights. It was because of one such fight that he was tragically killed. When Calamity Jane heard the news about her dear friend, she vowed to avenge his death, but she never found his killer.

Even though she missed Wild Bill, Calamity Jane was still as wild as ever. She was always full of surprises, and one of her greatest was when she began caring for smallpox victims. Smallpox was a terrible, deadly disease at the time, and many people were amazed that Calamity, who could be so wild and fierce, could also be gentle and loving with her patients. When she passed away, she asked to be buried next to her good friend, Wild Bill. To this day there are no two people who represented the ways of the Wild West better than Calamity Jane and Wild Bill Hickock.

From this valley they say you are going,
We will miss your bright eyes and sweet smile,
For they say you are taking the sunshine,
That brightens our pathway awhile.

Chorus
Come and sit by my side if you love me,
Do not hasten to bid me adieu,
But remember the Red River Valley,
And the girl that has loved you so true.

Red River Valley

Won't you think of the valley you're leaving?
Oh, how lonely, how sad it will be,
Oh think of the fond heart you're breaking,
And the grief you are causing me.

Chorus

From this valley they say you are going,
When you go, may your darling go, too?
Would you leave her behind unprotected
When she loves no other but you?

Chorus

I have promised you, darling, that never
Will a word from my lips cause you pain;
And my life, it will be yours forever
If you only will love me again.

from Ode to Immortality

BY WILLIAM WORDSWORTH

What though the radiance which was once so bright
Be now for ever taken from my sight,
Though nothing can bring back the hour
Of splendor in the grass, of glory in the flower,
We will grieve not, rather find
Strength in what remains behind;

A Fairy Tale Verse

Rip was a chap who relished fun,
And so when out with dog and gun
He came upon some little men
Who played at nine pins in a glen,
He joined them, drinking deep until
He slumbered, having had his fill.
When he awoke, his beard was gray;
His trusty dog had gone away;

Rip Van Winkle

Changed was the house he'd thought his own,
His children, men and women grown;
And he could scarce believe his ears
To learn he'd slept for twenty years.

There was an Old Man with a Beard

BY EDWARD LEAR

There was an Old Man with a beard,
Who said, 'It is just as I feared!—
Two Owls and a Hen, four Larks and a Wren,
Have all built their nests in my beard!'

There was an Old Man of Dumbree

BY EDWARD LEAR

There was an Old Man of Dumbree,
who taught little Owls to drink Tea;
For he said,
'To eat mice is not proper or nice,'
That amiable Man of Dumbree.

One-Dish Wonders

T he next time your grandchildren are over for dinner, surprise them with your quick kitchen finesse. Instead of ordering takeout chicken, Thai, or stir-fried rice, try these recipes for homemade substitutes that can be made faster than the time it takes for delivery. You can probably find most of the ingredients in your pantry already. In a half hour or less, you can have a hot meal on the table, with minimal cleanup. Now that's cooking, Grandpa-style!

Hoppin' John Supper

1 cup uncooked white rice
1 (15-ounce) can chicken broth
$1/4$ cup water
1 (16-ounce) package frozen
black-eyed peas, thawed
1 tablespoon vegetable oil
1 cup chopped onion
1 cup diced carrot
$3/4$ cup celery, thinly sliced, with tops
3 cloves garlic, minced)
12 ounces fully-cooked lean ham,
cut into $3/4$-inch cubes
1 teaspoon hot pepper sauce
$1/2$ teaspoon salt
2 tablespoons fresh chopped parsley

1. In large saucepan, combine rice, chicken broth, and water. Bring to a boil over high heat. Reduce heat and simmer, covered, for 10 minutes.
2. Stir in peas, then cover and simmer for 10 minutes more, or until peas are tender and liquid is absorbed.
3. In the meantime, heat oil in a large skillet over medium heat. Sauté onions, carrots, celery, and garlic for about 10 minutes, until vegetables are tender.
4. Add ham to veggies and heat through.
5. Stir in rice-and-bean mixture, pepper sauce, and salt.

6. Cover and cook over low heat for 10 minutes.
7. Sprinkle top with parsley and serve hot.

Makes 6 servings

Easy Thai Satay

1/2 cup creamy peanut butter
2 teaspoons lite soy sauce
2 teaspoons balsamic vinegar
1 tablespoon fresh lemon juice
1-ounce package of roasted-garlic salad dressing mix
3/4 cup water
1 pound sirloin, sliced and pounded thin
1 tablespoon sesame oil
Wooden skewers (presoaked in water to prevent them from scorching)

1. Preheat broiler.
2. In a small bowl, whisk together dipping sauce of peanut butter, soy sauce, vinegar, lemon juice, 1 tablespoon salad dressing mix, and water. Set aside.
3. In a large bowl, mix remaining salad dressing mix and sesame oil. Stir in sirloin strips until they are thoroughly coated.
4. Skewer each strip of beef and broil for 2 to 3 minutes per side.
5. Serve hot with the dipping sauce and enjoy!

Quick "Fried" Chicken

Nonstick vegetable spray
2 cups instant potato flakes
1 whole chicken, cut up, with skin removed, or 3 to 4 pounds chicken parts
1 cup ranch salad dressing

1. Preheat oven to 450°F.
2. Coat a baking sheet with nonstick vegetable spray.

3. Pour potato flakes onto a large plate or into a large bowl. Brush each piece of chicken with ranch dressing, then roll in potato flakes until completely coated.

4. Arrange chicken pieces on baking sheet and place in oven.
5. Turn oven down to 350º F and bake for 25 minutes, or until juices run clear when poked with a fork.

Makes 4 servings

Why the Sea Is Full of Salt

Once upon a time, there were two brothers who lived next to the ocean. One was very wealthy and had a gorgeous house overlooking the water, and the other was rather poor with just a little hut for himself and his extremely large family. Although the poor brother was a good man, he never seemed able to save any money, and was always borrowing things from his wealthy brother.

One day the poor brother really needed some money for medicine for one of his daughters. He was ashamed to ask his brother, but he didn't know where else to turn. He decided to ask his brother if he could exchange a ham he had for some money. He was walking slowly to his brother's house when he passed an old abandoned church. He heard lots of laughing and singing coming from inside.

"How strange," thought the brother. "I wonder what's going on." He went closer to investigate and met an old man with a long, white beard by the door.

"Good day," said the brother, and the old man returned his greeting. "What's going on in there?"

"It's a party," said the old man. "If you go in, all those inside will want to buy your ham, since they don't get meat very often. But you must not sell it for anything but a saltshaker that is behind the door."

"A saltshaker? Why would I want that?" asked the brother.

"It is magic. Whatever you wish for and then sprinkle with the magic salt will appear. When you get it, I will teach you the magic word to make it stop," said the old man.

The brother went inside with the ham, and just like the old man said, as soon as the people saw his ham they all tried to outbid each other to get it.

Why the Sea Is Full of Salt

"Well, I was going to trade the ham to my brother, but I will give it to you if you give me that saltshaker that sits behind the door," the brother told them.

At first they wouldn't hear of it, but gradually he wore them down, and finally they gave the saltshaker to the brother. When he left, the old man outside taught the brother the magic word that would make the saltshaker stop.

When he got back home, his wife was mad at him for staying out so late, but she was soon amazed when she saw him say the magic word, sprinkle a little of the salt, and have his daughter's medicine appear right before them! The brother said the magic word to make it stop, and his wife was overjoyed!

Then the brother shook out a delicious meal and the family had a very good time.

A few days went by, and the rich brother was amazed to realize his poor brother had not come by once to ask for anything. "I wonder what he is up to," he thought, and set out for his house.

Imagine his surprise when he came to it and saw beautiful curtains hanging from the windows and all new furniture inside! His poor brother welcomed him, and showed him all his new things that he had shaken from the magic saltshaker. At first he didn't want to tell his brother where he got the things, but after a while he finally revealed the truth.

"You must sell me that saltshaker!" cried the rich brother. "I will give you anything for it!"

"But it's very tricky, you have to say exactly the right—"

"I don't care!" cried his brother. "I need that saltshaker! I'll give you a hundred dollars for it! Five hundred! A thousand!"

Finally the brother agreed to sell him the saltshaker, not so much because he wanted the money, but because he could see how badly his brother wanted it.

Why the Sea Is Full of Salt

But before he could teach the brother the magic word to make it stop, the brother had grabbed the saltshaker and raced home.

There he set the saltshaker on his table. "What are you doing with that old thing?" asked his wife.

"It's a magic saltshaker. I just bought it from my brother. It can make anything!" he told her.

She snorted. "Ha! That thing probably can't even make salt! You've been tricked."

Angrily, the brother said the magic word to start the shaker, and wished for salt. Suddenly, streams of salt poured down from the shaker, and the wife was so stunned that she could hardly believe it! Soon there was enough salt to cover the entire table.

"All right," she declared, "I get it. Now, wish for something good, like caviar! Or lobster!"

But no matter how much the brother tried, he could not make the shaker stop making salt. Soon the floor of the kitchen was cov-ered with salt, and it didn't look like it was stopping.

His wife screamed, "If this keeps up, the whole world will be made of salt!"

Frantically, the brother dove through the salt, looking for the saltshaker. He just managed to pull it up through the mountain of salt in his house. He struggled over to the window, and using all of his might, threw the saltshaker as far out as he could. He saw it plummet down, down, down to the blue ocean and then—PLOP!— sink to the bottom, still making salt the whole time.

The brother looked around at the mess his house had become and began the difficult task of cleaning up. Luckily, his poor brother came along and helped him with it.

So, the magic saltshaker remains at the bottom of the sea to this day, still churning out salt. And this is why seawater has always tasted so salty.

The Old Dame & Her Maids

In olden times, before there were alarm clocks, an old lady kept a rooster in her yard, which would crow at dawn and wake her up each morning. The old lady then got up and woke her maids so that they could begin the day's work. The maids didn't like waking up so early in the morning, so one day they stole the rooster and left it far away from

the house. The next day, the old lady slept until very late because she did not hear the rooster crow. When she found out that the maids had driven the rooster away and she had no way of telling time, she woke the maids up ten times every night because she was afraid they would all oversleep. So instead of sleeping later, the maids got very little sleep!

Moral: What seems like the easy answer to a problem sometimes makes the problem worse.

On top of old Smoky,
All cover'd with snow,
I lost my true lover,
Come a-courtin' too slow.

A-courtin's a pleasure,
A-flirtin's a grief,
A false-hearted lover,
Is worse than a thief.

For a thief, he will rob you,
And take what you have,
But a false-hearted lover
Will send you to your grave.

She'll hug you and kiss you
And tell you more lies
Than the cross-ties on the railroad,
Or the stars in the skies.

On top of old Smoky,
All covered with snow,
I lost my true lover,
A-courtin' too slow.

On Top
of Old
Smoky

Gone Fishin'

The cooler's packed, the tackle box is full, and the fish are biting. What better way to spend a summer day than with your grandchildren on the lake, by the river, or at the ocean? With a little bit of bait and plenty of patience, even novice anglers can bring home the catch of the day. Even if you won't be having trout for dinner, a day spent fishing can be the most enjoyable way to do nothing at all. For beginners and seasoned salts alike, here are some tried and true methods to get more bites and keep the grandkids casting.

HOW TO GET HOOKED

- **STILL FISHING** is the basic "sit and wait" method, off a dock, pier, or rock. Putting weights, or "sinkers," on your line will help you catch fish that swim near the bottom; putting floats, or "bobbers" on your line makes it easier to hook fish near the surface.

- There are times when a moving lure, such as a wobbling spoon or spinner bait, will coax a fish into striking. With this type of fishing, called **CASTING**, you continually throw out and reel in your line.

- A combination of still fishing and casting, **TROLLING** is simply dragging a lure and/or live bait, off the back of a moving boat and waiting for the fish to bite.

- **FLY-FISHING** is the best way to catch fish that like to eat insects that hover near the water's surface, such as dragonflies. This type of fishing requires special lightweight lures, lines, rods, and reels. Instead of using bait, you tempt the fish with artificial flies, which are beautiful lifelike models made of fur, thread, feathers, and similar materials tied to a hook.

WHEN THE FISH AREN'T BITING

- *Try a different method.* If you've got a sinker on your line, switch to a bobber. If that doesn't work, try a spinner and cast for a while.
- *Move to a new spot.* You know the fish are in the lake, and sometimes you need to find them before they can find you.
- *Switch to a different kind of bait.* Try fish eggs instead of worms or grubs. If you're casting, try a different-colored lure. Try replacing you bait with a spinner.
- *Keep your eyes on other anglers who are reeling in fish.* What are they doing differently? Don't be shy about asking questions—but don't do this in the middle of the lake, as talking loudly will scare away fish! Most fishermen enjoy sharing their love for the sport. See if you can learn from their success.
- *Get your mind off fishing!* Read a book, see if you can spot other wildlife with binoculars, share stories (quietly) with your fishing partner, or play a card game.

Oftentimes, as soon as you forget about the fish, they'll come a-nibblin'.

Legendary Tall Tales: The Lost Treasure of Captain Kidd

Captain William Kidd was not having a good day. He was all set to leave Great Britain and sail back home to the American colonies. He had been transporting goods between the two continents for many months, and now he couldn't wait to get back and see his family. But just as he was getting ready to head off, two British soldiers stopped him and asked for a word with him. Then they made him an offer he couldn't refuse.

"William Kidd, how would you like to help out your mother country?" one asked.

"Depends on what you're asking," Kidd grumbled.

During the 1600s, pirates plagued the waters between the colonies and Great Britain. These bands of cutthroats stole riches and goods, slaughtered people, and forced others to join their murderous gangs.

The British government requested Captain Kidd become a pirate hunter. His job would be to sail up and down the eastern coast of America, attacking any pirate ship he saw.

Captain Kidd was not happy with this request. After all, he was only a simple sea captain and was eager to see his family again. But you couldn't just say no to the British king, and so Captain Kidd found himself reluctantly searching for pirates.

His crew wasn't very happy with the way things worked out either. "Why do we have to search for these bloody pirates?" his first mate, Smith asked.

"King's orders. Gotta do what the king says," Kidd answered.

"But we've been sailing for ages, and we haven't seen a single pirate ship."

The rest of the crew agreed, and Kidd

was afraid there would be a mutiny soon.

As the sun dipped below the horizon, they suddenly spotted a large ship in the distance. Kidd and his crew couldn't quite make out the flag, but everyone agreed that it looked like a pirate ship loaded with bounty. He reluctantly told the crew to open fire on the mysterious ship, and they soon captured it. But imagine their dismay when they realized that the ship was actually a member of the English fleet! Instead of protecting his country from pirates, Captain Kidd had accidentally become one!

He knew he'd be wanted for piracy if he returned to England, and that he'd be arrested immediately if he set foot in America. The only place left for him to go was Madagascar, a notorious pirate haven.

Captain Kidd knew he was in a terrible bind, but he didn't know what else to do. His crew convinced him that they might as well continue with their piracy, since they were already wanted men. And he was still angry with the British govern-

ment for putting him in this situation.

"I could've been home with my loving wife, curled up by the fire, enjoying a cup of chowder, and instead I'm out wandering the oceans, no better then a common cutthroat!" he told himself. And from that day forward, he and his crew captured many treasure-laden ships.

For a person who had begun his career as a law-abiding sea captain, Captain Kidd became quite the pirate. Within a few years his riches piled up, and his name was one of the most feared in the world. But money and riches didn't matter to him if he couldn't be with his family. He finally decided to sail for America and reunite with them.

The ship pulled along the coast of New Jersey, and Captain Kidd made his preparations to go ashore.

"Now, crew," he advised them, "I'm done with this life of piracy. We'll divide up the booty, and each man can go his own way. Agreed?" The crew gave their oaths, and the fabulous wealth was divvied up. Captain Kidd himself had two huge chests full of gold and jewels, which he buried in a secret location. Once he found his family, he would come back and reclaim his riches.

But this was not to be. When Captain Kidd arrived at his house, he found it empty. Although he knew he was a wanted man, he frantically ran to his neighbor's house to find out what happened. Imagine that man's surprise when he found the notorious Captain Kidd standing on his doorstep!

"No one knows what happened to your family, William," the man managed to gasp. "They didn't hear from you for so long that they thought you had died. One day, your wife and children packed up and left."

Captain Kidd was heartbroken and continued to search madly for his family, but no one knew where they had gone. Completely alone and miserable, he decided to give himself up to the local constables.

"After all, all the gold in the world is nothing if I don't have my family." He sighed.

Captain Kidd was arrested and sentenced to be executed. To this day, some people say you can still see his ghostly ship floating off the coast of Long Island and Cape May, New Jersey, still searching for the family he left long ago.

As for the fantastic riches he buried, no one has ever found them. Thousands of treasure-hunters have searched for the booty over the years. To this day the legendary treasure of Captain Kidd remains safely hidden, perhaps waiting for its ghostly owner to return and claim it once again. ⋏

Taco Temptations

Taco dinners make festive meals—and stuffing their own tortilla shells is ideal for picky eaters who like to play with their food! Traditional tacos often feature shredded or ground beef spiced up with taco seasoning, topped with shredded cheese, tomatoes, lettuce, olives, guacamole, and sour cream. Some of the following regional variations may be off the beaten path for many taco lovers, but once you try them, they might become the new standard at your dinner table.

SoCal Fish Tacos

$1/2$ cup sour cream
$1/2$ cup mayonnaise
$1/4$ cup cilantro, finely chopped
1 (1.25-ounce) package taco
seasoning mix
$1/8$ cup fresh-squeezed lime juice
1 pound cod fillets, cut into
1-inch pieces
2 tablespoons vegetable oil
2 tablespoons lemon juice
12 taco shells
$1^1/2$ cups shredded cabbage
2 tomatoes, chopped

1. In small bowl, whisk together sour cream, mayonnaise, cilantro, 2 tablespoons taco seasoning, and lime juice.
2. In medium bowl, stir cod pieces, oil, lemon juice, and remaining taco seasoning together. Pour contents into large skillet and cook over medium-high heat. Stir frequently for about 5 minutes, until fish flakes easily when tested with fork.
3. Fill taco shells with fish mixture and add cabbage and tomatoes Top with sour-cream blend. Serve immediately.

Makes 12 servings.

Southwestern Chicken Tacos

Nonstick cooking spray
12 ounces chicken breast,
cut into small pieces
1 cup salsa
1 (7-ounce) can Mexican-style
corn, drained
1/2 cup canned black beans, drained
8 taco shells
1 1/2 cups shredded lettuce
1/2 cup shredded cheddar cheese or
Mexican white cheese
1 tomato, chopped
Sour cream

1. Coat large skillet with cooking spray and heat over medium flame. Add chicken and 1/2 cup salsa, and cook for about 5 minutes, stirring frequently, until chicken is cooked through.
2. Stir in corn and beans, and simmer for about 3 minutes, until mixture is slightly reduced.
3. Spoon chicken mixture into taco shells. Top with lettuce, cheese, tomato, and remaining salsa. Add a dollop of sour cream, if desired.

Makes 8 servings

Picadillo Salsa

3 large ripe tomatoes, cored
and chopped
1 medium red onion, chopped
1/2 bunch cilantro, finely chopped
3 jalapeño peppers, cored and finely
chopped (you might want to wear
gloves for this to avoid getting
pepper juice on skin)
1/4 cup fresh-squeezed lime juice
Sea salt to taste

1. In medium-size bowl, stir all ingredients together until blended.
2. Adjust ingredients to personal taste and serve with tacos or as dip for tortilla chips.

Makes about 2 cups

Very Veggie Tacos

1 tablespoon vegetable oil
1 medium onion, thinly sliced
1 green pepper, thinly sliced
1 hot serrano pepper, thinly sliced (you might want to wear gloves for this to avoid getting pepper juice on skin)
1 medium zucchini, thinly sliced
1/2 cup water
1 clove garlic, minced
2 1/2 cups beans (black, refried, or pinto)
1 large tomato, chopped
Sea salt to taste
8 taco shells
Sour cream
Taco sauce

1. In large skillet, sauté onion and peppers in hot oil over medium heat until tender.
2. Add zucchini and cook for about 5 minutes more.
3. Add 1/4 cup water and garlic. Bring mixture to a simmer.
4. Add beans and remaining water and bring mixture to a boil.
5. When mixture is heated through and has reached desired consistency, remove from heat. Stir in tomatoes. Add salt to taste.
6. Spoon veggie mixture into taco shells. Garnish each with dollop of sour cream and dash of taco sauce, if desired.

Makes 8 servings

Ocean Tide-Pooling

Spending a day at the beach can open a world of discovery for young explorers. Low tide reveals the otherwise hidden homes of anemones, hermit crabs, and other sea creatures. When you take your grandchildren trolling along rocky coastlines, see how many different life forms you can identify. In bigger tide-pool areas, you can make your own undersea dredge for seeing things up close. Encourage your grandchildren to tread lightly on fragile coastal areas: What may look like dried up seaweed could rally back to life when the tide rolls in again.

DRYING RACK

24- x 24-inch wooden board or shallow wooden crate (such as a fruit crate from the grocery), tacks

A day tide-pooling might yield an interesting assortment of kelp, sea squirts, hermit crabs, or starfish. The best way to preserve your collection is to spread it on a flat surface in the sun until completely dried out. Use tacks to pin starfish into shape or spread out seaweed.

SEASHORE DREDGE

Small plastic pail with handle, fine-mesh sack (such as onion or potato sacking from the grocery), twine, box cutter or knife, rope

Grandchildren can use a simple dredge along the edges of tide pools or along the ocean floor and get an up-close look at sea life. Cut the bottom out of a plastic bucket and punch several holes around the middle to attach the sack. Through the holes, fasten the sack to the bucket with twine. Tie a line of rope to the handle for dredging off piers or in deep tide pool areas.

Seashore Scenery

■ **LIMPETS** are conical shells commonly found clinging to tidal rocks and seaweeds. They vary in color and often have iridescent interiors.

■ **ROCK SHELLS** and **WHELKS** are the homes of carnivorous snails, commonly found among rocks or pebbly areas at low tide.

■ **SEA ANEMONES** inhabit tide pools, where they attach themselves to the base of rocks or use their tentacles to anchor themselves in the sand.

■ **STARFISH** can often be found in lower tide pools or along open rocky shores, where they feed on shellfish and barnacles.

■ Abundant along high-tide rocks, **BARNACLES** may look like dead crusty formations, but look for their feeding movements under water at high tide.

■ **HERMIT CRABS** like to burrow into muddy coastal flats or upper tide-pool regions.

The Child & The Brook

An old man who saw a child stand for a long time by the side of a stream, said, "My child, why do you gaze so long on this brook?" "Sir," said the child, "I stay here to wait until the stream has dried up, for then I can pass with dry feet." "No." The old man chuckled. "You might wait here your entire life and yet not do that, for this brook will run on as long as time. And as you grow up, you will find this out. Either follow the stream to get to sea or get your feet wet!"

Moral: It's better to be active than to wait for things to happen.

Do not go gentle into that good night,
Old age should burn and rave at close of day;
Rage, rage against the dying of the light.

Though wise men at their end know dark is right,
Because their words had forked no lightning they
Do not go gentle into that good night.

Good men, the last wave by, crying how bright
Their frail deeds might have danced in a green bay,
Rage, rage against the dying of the light.

Wild men who caught and sang the sun in flight,
And learn, too late, they grieved it on its way,
Do not go gentle into that good night.

Do Not Go Gentle into That Good Night

BY DYLAN THOMAS

Grave men, near death, who see with blinding sight
Blind eyes could blaze like meteors and be gay,
Rage, rage against the dying of the light.

And you, my father, there on the sad height,
Curse, bless, me now with your fierce tears, I pray.
Do not go gentle into that good night.
Rage, rage against the dying of the light.

A Fairy Tale Verse

You know the puss of clever pate
Who made his master rich and great:
First to the king he sent some game
And tagged it with his master's name;
Then when the king was passing by,
"These are my *master's* fields!" he'd cry;
A giant (in disguise a mouse)
He ate, and seized the giant's house,

Puss in Boots

Where, boasting it his lord's domain
The king he begged to entertain.
All this, of course, was sure to please,
And Puss, henceforward, lived in ease.

THE LITTLE PRINCE

by Antoine de Saint-Exupéry

It was then that the fox appeared.

"Good morning," said the fox.

"Good morning," the little prince answered politely, though when he turned around he saw nothing.

"I'm here," the voice said, "under the apple tree."

"Who are you?" the little prince asked. "You're very pretty . . ."

"I'm a fox," the fox said.

"Come and play with me," the little prince proposed. "I'm feeling so sad."

"I can't play with you," the fox said. "I'm not tamed."

"Ah! Excuse me," said the little prince. But upon reflection he added, "What does *tamed* mean?"

"You're not from around here," the fox said. "What are you looking for?"

"I'm looking for people," said the little prince. "What does *tamed* mean?"

"People," said the fox, "have guns and they hunt. It's quite troublesome. And they also raise chickens. That's the only interesting thing about them. Are you looking for chickens?"

"No," said the little prince, "I'm looking for friends. What does *tamed* mean?"

"It's something that's been too often neglected. It means, 'to create ties' . . ."

"'To create ties'?"

"That's right," the fox said. "For me you're only a little boy just like a hundred thousand other little boys. And I have no need of you. And you have no need of me, either. For you I'm only a fox like a hundred thousand other foxes. But if you tame me, we'll need each other. You'll be the only boy in the world for me. I'll be the only fox in the world for you . . ."

"I'm beginning to understand," the little prince said. "There's a flower . . . I think she's tamed me . . ."

"Possibly," the fox said. "On Earth, one sees all kinds of things."

"Oh, this isn't on Earth," the little prince said.

The fox seemed quite intrigued. "On another planet?"

"Yes."

"Are there hunters on that planet?"

"No."

"Now that's interesting. And chickens?"

"No."

"Nothing's perfect," sighed the fox. But he returned to his idea. "My life is monotonous. I hunt chickens; people hunt me. All chickens are just alike, and all men are just alike. So I'm rather bored. But if you tame me, my life will be filled with sunshine. I'll know the sound of foot-

324

steps that will be different from all the rest. Other footsteps send me back underground. Yours will call me out of my burrow like music. And then, look! You see the wheat fields over there? I don't eat bread. For me wheat is of no use whatever. Wheat fields say nothing to me. Which is sad. But you have hair the color of gold. So it will be wonderful, once you've tamed me! The wheat, which is golden, will remind me of you. And I'll love the sound of the wind in the wheat . . ."

The fox fell silent and stared at the little prince for a long while. "Please . . . tame me!" he said.

"I'd like to," the little prince replied, "but I haven't much time. I have friends to find and so many things to learn."

"The only things you learn are the things you tame," said the fox. "People haven't time to learn anything. They buy things ready-made in stores. But since there are no stores where you can buy friends, people no longer have friends. If you want a friend, tame me!"

"What do I have to do?" asked the little prince.

"You have to be very patient," the fox answered. "First you'll sit down a little ways away from me, over there, in the grass. I'll watch you out of the corner of my eye, and you won't say anything. Language is the source of misunderstandings. But day by day, you'll be able to sit a little closer . . ."

Refrigerator Cakes

There's something sweet and delectable about taking an afternoon to bake a traditional cake using old-fashioned ingredients just like your grandparents used to. Nevertheless, making homemade cakes and pies doesn't have to take all day: There's always a secret shortcut for something delicious. Making the best cakes doesn't require an oven—the refrigerator will do just fine. These desserts are simple to make and are yummy with a glass of milk.

Pineapple Crunch Cake

1 (1/4-ounce) package plain gelatin
1/2 cup confectioners' sugar
1/4 cup butter, room temperature
1 egg yolk, beaten
1/2 cup crushed pineapple
1/4 cup chopped walnuts
1 egg white, whipped until stiff
18 graham crackers
Whipped cream as garnish

1. Prepare gelatin using package directions and set aside to cool.
2. In large bowl, mix sugar, butter, and beaten egg yolk together. Stir in pineapple and walnuts and blend well. Fold in egg white.
3. In a 9-x 11-inch baking dish spread a layer of graham crackers so they fit snugly along the bottom.
4. Top with filling and chill 4 hours in refrigerator until cake is set.
5. Serve with a dollop of cream.

Makes 6 to 8 servings

Strawberry Orange Cake

1 (12-ounce) package ladyfingers
4 cups fresh orange juice
1 1/2 cups sugar
3 (1/4-ounce) packages plain gelatin
1/3 cup fresh-squeezed lemon juice
1/8 teaspoon salt
1 cup heavy whipping cream

1 cup diced orange segments
2 cups fresh strawberries, sliced

1. Split ladyfingers in half and layer them on the bottom of an 8-inch springform pan.
2. In small saucepan, stir 1 cup orange juice and sugar over medium heat until sugar dissolves. Remove from heat.
3. In separate bowl, dissolve gelatin in 1 cup orange juice. Stir into hot juice. Add remaining orange juice, lemon juice, and salt to hot juice and stir. Chill until mixture thickens slightly.
4. Whip cream until stiff and fold in to juice mixture. Fold in orange segments.
5. Spoon mixture over ladyfingers and chill for about 4 hours.
6. Arrange sliced strawberries in decorative circular pattern on top.
7. Remove springform sides and place cake on serving platter.

Makes 6 to 8 servings

Chocolate Cake

2 cups heavy whipping cream
$1/4$ cup chocolate syrup
1 package chocolate graham crackers
or chocolate wafers

1. Chill bowl and beaters in freezer for $1/2$ hour.
2. In chilled bowl, whip cream until stiff peaks form. Slowly beat in chocolate syrup.
3. Layer bottom of 12- x 8-inch glass pan with graham crackers or wafers. Add $1/2$-inch layer of chocolate cream. Repeat layering with cookies and cream until pan is full.
4. Chill 4 hours in refrigerator before cutting into squares and serving.

Makes about 12 servings

Grandfather Wisdoms

Everything comes to him who hustles while he waits.

—THOMAS EDISON

■

Never give in, never give in, never, never, never,
never—in nothing great or small, large or petty—
never give in except to convictions of honor
and good sense.

—WINSTON CHURCHILL

■

A journey of a thousand miles
begins with a single step.

—LAO-TZU

■

Everyone has inside of him a piece of good
news. The good news is that you don't
know how great you can be!

—ANNE FRANK

The greatest accomplishment is not in never falling, but in rising again after you fall.
—VINCE LOMBARDI

■

If at first you don't succeed, try, try, try again.
—W. E. HICKSON

■

You may encounter many defeats, but you must not be defeated.
—MAYA ANGELOU

■

When you get to the end of your rope, tie a knot and hang on.
—FRANKLIN D. ROOSEVELT

LEGENDARY TALL TALES: DANIEL BOONE AND THE GREAT OUTDOORS

One of the great outdoorsman of America was a man named Daniel Boone. Daniel was born in Pennsylvania around 1734. Some say he had ten brothers and sisters! With that many children running around the house, was it any wonder he spent a lot of his time in the great outdoors? He learned how to hunt and gather and survive off the land at a young age. Never one to back down from a challenge, he was always fascinated by stories of adventures from the unexplored areas of America.

When he got a little older, he met an experienced scout named John Finley. Finley loved to tell stories, especially about a wondrous land over the Appalachian Mountains called Kentucky.

"Why, the hills roll on forever," he told the young Daniel Boone, "There's plenty of space for a man to spread out!"

Daniel considered his crowded household and knew that Kentucky was just the place for him. But he also knew that it would take every ounce of his strength and courage to tame that rugged land. Daniel prepared for this challenge by sharpening his tracking and hunting skills all the way from Pennsylvania to North Carolina. When he finally decided he was ready to tackle Kentucky, he joined a party of five men, including his old friend John Finley. They set off west through the Cumberland Gap, a notoriously treacherous path with steep cliffs.

The tough journey stretched on for days and days, but they finally made it to the beautiful, fertile land of Kentucky.

Daniel loved Kentucky so much that he moved his family there and carved out a path called Wilderness Trail so it would be easier for others to settle.

Daniel Boone continued to explore uncharted areas and used his fantastic outdoor skills to carve a niche out of the rugged landscape. Pioneers said Daniel was such a good tracker and scout that he had the eyes of an eagle and a memory as long as a river.

One time, Daniel found a beautiful area in a forest where the fish practically leaped onto your fishhook, and the leaves turned as bright as gold in the sun. He cut three notches into a young oak tree sapling nearby to mark the spot so he could return to it later on.

Twenty years later, Daniel remembered this special spot and told his friends about it.

"Daniel, that was over two decades ago." They all laughed. "You think you can find this place again because of some little scratches on a tree trunk?"

"I don't *think* I

can, I *know* I can!" Daniel declared, and they organized a party to search for it. The group followed Daniel through the wild areas until finally he came to a stop beneath a tall group of trees.

"This is definitely the place," Daniel told them. His friends checked the trees and then began to laugh.

"Daniel, you fool," one said, "there's no marked tree here!" Daniel Boone studied one of the trees carefully, and then took his knife out and gently scraped off a bit of moss that had grown on the trunk. There, plain as day, were the three marks Daniel had cut into the trunk those many years ago. Daniel Boone had done it, and no one doubted his tracking skills ever again. 🏃

Into the Woods

As every scouting grandfather knows, the secret to camping success is having good foresight. Pitching a perfect tent has less to do with the kind of tent you have and more to do with where you pitch it. By looking for potential troubles ahead of time, you can avoid them in the middle of the night. Similar principals apply to building campfires. With proper preparation, you can build one that will light right away, burn for hours, and last longer than the best ghost story ever told.

THE BEST TENT SPOT EVER

Even if your grandchildren aren't yet able to put up a tent by themselves, they can still do the most important part: picking and prepping the right spot. Here's how:

1. Choose a camping area away from stagnant pools of water, where mosquitoes may be breeding.

2. Scout the area for signs of animal activity, such as anthills, burrows, droppings, or tracks. Avoid pitching your tent on or near these, as you may receive unwanted visitors after the tent is up.

3. Survey the surface for a dry, flat, and even patch of bare ground.

4. Clear away pinecones, rocks, twigs, leaves, and similar loose ground cover.

5. Note the direction of the wind. If the tent door opens to the wind, unwanted rain and debris can blow easily into the tent.

6. Avoid pitching your tent in an open area or on top of a hill. These areas can be excessively windy and cause your tent to blow over.

7. Look out for low-hanging tree branches

that might drop sap, dew, pollen, or leaves on your tent.

8. Note which direction is east. You may not want the rising sun to shine directly in your window or door first thing in the morning.

THE FOUR-STEP ONE-MATCH CAMPFIRE

For best results, keep a long poker stick nearby and a bucket of water for emergency dousing.

1. **CLEAR** a circular area that will serve as your fire pit. If possible, arrange a ring of large stones around the circle to enclose the pit.

2. **GATHER** three types of materials: fine kindling, medium-size sticks, and large logs.

Kindling should be dry and brittle. Use such items as pinecones and needles, balled up newspaper, twigs, and leaves.

3. **STACK** a small pile of kindling in the fire pit. Arrange the sticks around the kindling in the shape of a tepee, with smaller pieces on the inside and larger pieces on the outside. Finally, lean three or four logs against the tepee. Be sure to leave room for air to circulate between the branches.

4. **LIGHT** the fire by striking a match and holding it at a downward angle to protect the flame from extinguishing. Light the kindling first by pushing the match through a space in the logs into the middle, then gently blow on the flames until they catch on the sticks. Then sit back, relax, and enjoy the flickering flames. Continue to add additional logs to the fire as the fire dies down.

Never leave a campfire unattended. When you're ready to turn in for the night, be sure to put out the fire completely with water. Then stir the ashes and douse with more water.

Stopping by Woods on a Snowy Evening

BY ROBERT FROST

Whose woods these are I think I know.
His house is in the village though;
He will not see me stopping here
To watch his woods fill up with snow.

My little horse must think it queer
To stop without a farmhouse near
Between the woods and frozen lake
The darkest evening of the year.

He gives his harness bells a shake
To ask if there is some mistake.
The only other sound's the sweep
Of easy wind and downy flake.

The woods are lovely, dark, and deep.
But I have promises to keep,
And miles to go before I sleep,
And miles to go before I sleep.

Simple Camp Cooking

One of the best things about making the perfect campfire is the mouthwatering smell of campfire cooking. Whether heading out for an early fishing expedition or hike through the woods, sunrise hearty hash is sure to please the taste buds and give you a good head start on the day. Chuckwagon burgers cook in minutes, and with the added cornchips in the mix, buns are optional. Sweet, fresh summer corn is cooked to perfection over hot coals, and the best part is that it comes in its own cooking wrapper. And as the campfire dies down into a golden glow, it becomes just the right temperature for making yummy roasted-apple pockets.

Sunrise Hearty Hash

2 large potatoes
1 onion
Water
1 tablespoon mustard
Salt, to taste
Pepper, to taste
A few dashes Tabasco sauce
1 12-ounce can corned beef
4 eggs, cooked sunny side up

1. Dice the potatoes and onions and combine in a large skillet. Add enough water to cover the potatoes and onions, and stir in mustard, salt, pepper, Tabasco sauce.
2. Allow the mixture to simmer over medium coals until almost tender.
3. Stir in the corned beef and adjust the seasonings if necessary. Continue to simmer uncovered until the mixture is tender and of the desired consistency.
4. Serve on a platter and top with a sunny-side-up egg.

Makes 4 servings

Chuckwagon Burgers

1½ pounds ground beef, ground
turkey, or veggie burger
1 cup corn chips, crushed
1 egg
1 tablespoon chili powder
1 teaspoon ground cumin
½ teaspoon salt

1. Combine all ingredients in a large bowl and mix until well blended.
2. Divide into four balls and shape into patties.
3. Grill over medium coals about 4 to 6 minutes per side until burgers are browned and the middle is no longer pink.

Makes 4 servings

Campfire Corn

Corn on the cob, with husks
Water
Butter, to taste
Salt, to taste
Herb seasoning, to taste

1. Pull back the leafy husks of the corn just enough to pull out the silky strands. Wrap the leaves over the ears again and soak the corncobs in a large pot of water.
2. Shake the excess water off the corncobs and place them on top of the edges of hot coals.
3. Allow them to cook for about 15 minutes, then use tongs to remove them from the coals.
4. Test the readiness with a fork: when a pricked kernel is soft enough to eat, allow the corn to cool, then peel back the husks, and eat plain, or rub with a little butter, herbs, or salt to taste.

Roasted Apple Pockets

Apples, whole
2 tablespoons raisins per apple
1 teaspoon brown sugar per apple
¹/₂ teaspoon cinnamon per apple
Aluminum foil

1. With a paring knife, core each apple, but save a bit of the top with the stem intact, jack-o'-lantern-style.
2. Fill the center with raisins, brown sugar, and cinnamon, then replace the apple's top.
3. Wrap each apple in aluminum foil and set atop the dying embers for about 15 minutes.
3. Remove the apple with tongs, and when foil has cooled enough to touch, bite into the gooey hot apple, or enjoy with a spoon.

Oh, give me a home, where the buffalo roam,
Where the deer and the antelope play;
Where seldom is heard a discouraging word,
And the skies are not cloudy all day.

Chorus
Home, home on the range,
Where the deer and the antelope play;
Where seldom is heard a discouraging word,
And the skies are not cloudy all day.

How often at night when the heavens are bright
With the lights from the glittering stars;
Have I stood there amazed and asked as I gazed
If their glory exceeds that of ours.

Chorus

Oh, give me a land where the bright diamond sand
Flows leisurely down the stream;
Where the graceful, white swan goes gliding along,
Like a maid in a heavenly dream.

Chorus

Where the air is so pure, the zephyrs so free,
The breezes so balmy and light,

Home On the Range

That I would not exchange my home on
the range
For all of the cities so bright.

Chorus

Oh, I love those wild flowers in this dear land of ours,
The curlew I love to hear scream,
And I love the white rocks and the antelope flocks
That graze on the mountain tops green.

Chorus

A Fairy Tale Verse

Two little children, dear and good,
Were sent to wander in the wood,
Because their uncle, bad and bold,
Desired to seize their goods and gold;
For since they seemed so sweet and pretty
He spared their young lives out of pity.
Afraid, for days they trudged about
Till hungry, cold, and quite tired out,

Babes in the Wood

Within the lonesome forest deep
The babes lay down and fell asleep,
And then the kindly robins spread
A quilt of leaves upon their bed.

The Star Dipper

Near the deep dark woods, there stood a little house. It was a very little house, but it was big enough for a little girl and her mother.

One summer night the little girl's mother did not feel well. She tossed about on her bed and could not go to sleep.

"I am so thirsty," she said. "I wish I had a drink of cold water."

The little girl was very kind and thoughtful.

"I will get you a drink, Mother," she said. She jumped out of bed and slipped on her dress and shoes. She took an old tin dipper and ran out to the well in the yard. She pulled up the bucket, but not a drop of water was in it. The well was dry.

"What shall I do?" said the kind little girl. "It is so warm and Mother is so thirsty. She must have a drink of nice cold water. I will go to the spring. There will

surely be some water there."

Now the spring was a long way off in the woods and it was a very dark night.

"I must try hard not to be afraid," said the kind little girl.

She ran down the dark road and took the path into the woods. It was still darker in the woods. She could not see the path and soon she had lost her way.

The sharp little stones cut through her thin shoes. She tumbled over the big stones. The branches of the trees caught her dress and tore it. But she did not turn back.

"Oh! where is the spring?" cried the little girl. "I must find it. Mother is so very thirsty."

At last she heard a little trickling sound. She knew then she had found the spring. She knelt down and filled the old tin dipper. Then she started back home carrying it very carefully.

Soon she met a little dog. He

was panting and his pink tongue was hanging out of his mouth.

"Poor little dog," thought the kind little girl, "he must be very thirsty. The brooks are all dry."

"Little dog," she said aloud. "I will give you a drink of this cold water. I have filled the dipper for my mother, but there is enough for you too."

She poured some of the water into her hand and the little dog lapped it up eagerly. How good it tasted! He gave two sharp little barks to say thank you.

Then the little girl noticed that it had grown lighter. The light seemed to come from her hand. She looked down and saw that the old tin dipper had turned to silver. It was bright and shining like the silver moon.

Now the little girl could see her way plainly. She could walk much faster with the help of the silvery light from the dipper.

After a while she met an old man.

"Little girl," he asked, "can you tell me where I can get a drink of cold water? The brooks are all dry and I cannot find a spring. I am very thirsty and tired."

"I will give you a drink," said the kind little girl. And she gave him some of the cold water from her silver dipper.

"Thank you, kind little girl," said the old man. "Now I can go on my way."

And he said good-bye to the kind little girl.

As soon as he was out of sight, she noticed that it had grown even lighter than before. She looked down and saw that the silver dipper had turned to gold. It was very bright indeed and shone like the golden sun.

The kind little girl could see even better than before, so that it was not long before she reached home.

"I have brought you a drink of cold water from the spring," said the good little girl and she handed the golden dipper to her mother. How good the clear, cold water tasted! She drank and drank until there was not a drop left in the golden dipper.

"Thank you for going to the spring, my good little girl," said the mother. "Now I feel much better. I shall be able to get up in the morning and do my work."

Then the good little girl and her mother noticed strange, bright lights flashing on the walls of the little house. They looked down at the golden dipper. Something very wonderful had happened.

The golden dipper had changed to sparkling diamonds.

Out of the window went the diamonds and up, up into the sky. The kind little girl and her mother stood in the doorway watching. In the sky the diamonds turned to seven bright, twinkling stars. They made a dipper in the sky.

The kind little girl and her mother lived many years ago, but if you look up into the sky some bright, starry night, you will see the dipper still there.

When you see it, think about the kind little girl, who was brave enough to go into the dark woods alone.

Star Sense

The nighttime can be frightening for young children, especially when darkness and shadows conceal the world as they know it in the daytime. But with some special tips on how to use the stars to their advantage, children can not only overcome nervousness about the dark, but actually look forward to using their newfound nocturnal abilities. On the next clear, starry night you spend with your grandchildren, share these fun secrets about the stars and see how they improve their star sense.

KNOW HOW FAR NORTH YOU ARE

On a clear night, you can show your grandchildren the same star by which mariners have navigated since ancient times. Polaris, also called the Pole Star or the North Star, is easy to spot once you locate the Big Dipper. If you follow a line through the outer two stars of the Big Dipper's "ladle" (Merak and Dubhe), it will point to Polaris, the first star in the "handle" of the Little Dipper.

Once your grandchildren locate Polaris, they can use a hand as a measuring device to determine how far north of the equator they're standing. When you hold your hand

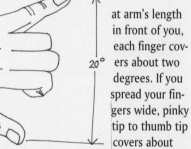

20°

at arm's length in front of you, each finger covers about two degrees. If you spread your fingers wide, pinky tip to thumb tip covers about twenty degrees. Using your hand, measure the degrees between the horizon and the North Star. There are 69 miles in a degree. So, to calculate the number of miles north of the equator you're standing, simply multiply the number of degrees by 69.

LISTEN TO A FALLING STAR

Stargazing is always fun during meteor showers when you can spend the night counting falling stars. But what if there's cloud cover? No problem—there's more than one way to catch a falling star. Just tune in to an FM radio and instead of watching meteors fall, you and your grandchildren can listen to them. A meteor leaves a trail of ions as it falls. These particles register as *pings* that sound like a tone, a bit of music, or static on FM stations. With an FM/TV antenna, you can best catch these *pings* on a radio tuned between 88 and 108 MHz.

IMPROVE YOUR NIGHT VISION

You and your grandchildren may not have night vision goggles or the keen eyesight of a nocturnal critter, but you can still learn how to see better in the dark. The secret is to use an old astronomer's trick called "averted vision." On a clear night when you can see the stars, simply look off to one side of the object that you're viewing. After doing this for a while, you'll notice that the object will appear brighter than when looking at it directly. Explain to your grandchildren the reason for this has to do with the design of our eyes. When we look at something directly, we are using the iris, made of cone cells, which allow us to see better in bright light.

When we look at something off-center, we're taking advantage of our rod cells, which allow us to see better in the dark.

Another way to see the stars better at night is by using a sighting tube. Any long, cylindrical tube, such as a cardboard tube for a poster or wrapping paper, can become a sighting tube. Simply cup one eye with your hand and peer into the sky through the tube with the other eye. The sighting tube will cut down on nearby light pollution from streetlights or a campfire and can make dim stars appear brighter.

I've often thought

How nice the big
new moon would be
For little me to
sit in.
'Twould be a cozy
rocking chair
That sleepy me
would fit in.

But if the moon
got very full
And just a little
frisky,
Perhaps my cozy
rocking chair
Would be a little
risky.

ACKNOWLEDGMENTS

"On Ageing" copyright © 1978 by Maya Angelou, from *And Still I Rise* by Maya Angelou. Used by permission of Random House, Inc.

From *Charlie and the Chocolate Factory* by Roald Dahl, copyright © 1964, renewed 1992 by Roald Dahl Nominee Limited. Used by permission of Alfred A. Knopf, an imprint of Random House Children's Books, a division of Random House, Inc.

"Leisure" from *The Complete Poems of W.H. Davies* (Jonathan Cape Ltd, 1940) by permission of the Executors of the W.H. Davies Estate and Random House UK Ltd.

From *The Black Stallion* by Walter Farley, copyright © 1941 by Walter Farley. Copyright renewed 1969 by Walter Farley. Used by permission of Random House Children's Books, a division of Random House, Inc.

"Stopping by Woods on a Snowy Evening" from *The Poetry of Robert Frost* edited by Edward Connery Latham. Copyright © 1923, 1969 by Henry Holt and Company, copyright © 1951 by Robert Frost. Reprinted by permission of Henry Holt and Company, LLC.

"As I Grew Older" and "Still Here" from *The Collected Poems of Langston Hughes* by Langston Hughes, copyright © 1994 by The Estate of Langston Hughes. Used by permission of Alfred A. Knopf, a division of Random House, Inc.

"Big Little Boy" from *Catch A Little Rhyme* by Eve Merriam. Copyright © 1966 Eve Merriam. Copyright © renewed Dee Michel and Guy Michel. Used by permission of Marian Reiner.

"Surprise!" by Shel Silverstein. Copyright © 1981 by Evil Eye Music, Inc. Used by permission of HarperCollins Publishers.

"Do Not Go Gentle into That Good Night" By Dylan Thomas, from *The Poems of Dylan Thomas,* copyright © 1952 by Dylan Thomas. Reprinted by permission of New Directions Publishing Corp.

Excerpt from *The Little Prince* by Antoine de Saint-Exupéry, copyright © 1943 by Harcourt, Inc. and renewed 1971 by Consuelo de Saint-Exupéry, English translation copyright © 2000 by Richard Howard, reprinted by permission of Harcourt, Inc.

Submitted excerpt from *A Tree Grows in Brooklyn* by Betty Smith. Copyright 1943, 1947 by Betty Smith. Copyright renewed 1971 by Betty Smith (Finch). Reprinted by permission of HarperCollins Publishers Inc.

Two haiku by Kobayashi Issa: "Even with insect-some sing, some can't", p. 155 and "Climb Mount Fuji, O snail, But slowly, slowly", p. 163, from *The Essential Haiku: Versions of Basho, Buson & Issa, Edited and with an Introduction by Robert Hass*. Introduction and selection copyright © 1994 by Robert Hass. Unless otherwise noted, all translations copyright © 1994 by Robert Hass. Reprinted by permission of HarperCollins Publishers Inc.

ILLUSTRATIONS

pg. 1: Charles Moritz; 3, 36, 41, 120, 229, 233, 244, 316, 323, 345: Jessie Willcox Smith; pg. 13-14: Frank Hart; pg. 31: J.R. Shaver; pg. 32-33, 327: C. Twelvetrees; pg. 39, 73, 89, 143, 171, 173, 196, 286, 320, 342: C. M. Burd; pg. 60, 65: W. W. Denslow; pg. 68-69: Flora Adele Nash; pg. 101: B. Cory Kilvert; pg. 134, 184: Miriam Story Hurford; pg. 154-155: F. N. Donaldson; pg. 169: H.Y. Hintermeister; p. 175: E. Curtis; pg. 176-177: Shel Silverstein; pg. 194, 260: N. Dowdall; pg. 198-199: John Gee; pg. 207: Alan Foster; pg. 223, 224: Ruth E. Newton; pg. 234: Frank E. Schoonover; pg. 239: Florence Hardy; pg. 249: Jacob Bates Abbott; pg. 255: Mabel Udvardy; pg. 257, 263: Harrison Cady; pg. 264: Lilian Rowles; pg. 269, 272: L. Leslie Brooke; pg. 278: John Held Jr.; pg. 284-285: Barham; pg. 291: CA Brule; pg. 293: Francis Brundage; pg. 303: Norman Rockwell; pg. 307: Ekman; pg. 309: Jim Glackens; pg. 314-315: M. L. Clements; pg. 329: Georges Redon; pg. 333: A. E. Marty; pg. 337: Hazel Frazee; pg. 339: Margaret Evans Price.